Holiday Rogue

AN ALBERTINI FAMILY ROMANCE

THE ANNA ALBERTINI FILES
BOOK 4.5

REBECCA ZANETTI

RAZ INK LLC

This special edition is dedicated to everyone attending Readers Take Denver 2024 for jumping in and having some fun with this Albertini Family. I hope you enjoy this special edition made just for you.

One Cursed Rose

Hi there! Thanks for attending Readers Take Denver with all of us! I'm happy to provide a fun novella for you to read and wanted to make sure you knew about a new series I have debuting on June 25, 2024 called GRIMM BARGAINS.

The first book, One Cursed Rose, is a dark retelling of Beauty and the Beast within the high-stakes world of social media that runs on crystals. It's sexy, intriguing, and fun - and I hope you like it!

EXCERPT from One Cursed Rose:

Alana

Panic stifles a scream in my throat. Somehow, this impossibly strong man has an arm around my legs as he runs through what appears to be a storage area and kicks open a door. Then we're running through abusive rain. I'm tossed into the back of an SUV and I roll over, my shoulders hitting the far side. The man jumps inside. "Go," he snaps.

The driver punches the gas, and we speed off down the alley-way. I scramble and sit up, trying to blink and focus my eyes in the darkened interior. "Who are you?"

The man turns toward me. Everything inside me goes quiet before exploding tumultuously alive. Even with a jagged scar that runs from his forehead, through his left eyebrow, and across the bridge of his nose to the other cheekbone, he is by far the most handsome man I've ever seen.

His mere presence is a warning as he takes up more than his fair share of the back seat. In comparison with the men in the bar I just left, he wears a rough black leather jacket, ripped and faded jeans, and battered but high end combat boots. Rain dots his thick black hair, making it curl slightly beneath his ears. The breath of his shoulders alone intimidate me, and that's before I notice the blood on his neck and the bruises on his knuckles.

So I turn, facing him, pulling one leg up on the seat in case I need to pivot on my knee and attack him. The difference in our sizes makes that idea stupid. But I know letting any kidnapper take you away from a public space is a death sentence.

"Who are you?" My voice trembles this time. His eyes are black with, I swear, flicks of silver. Not gold, not brown, not amber, but silver. I have never seen the color before, but I know those eyes. "You've been watching me." I flash back to the other night across the street.

"You're very watchable," he says, his voice deep and rich like a McMillan Sherry Oak 18 year old scotch. So he does not deny it.

I'm not sure if that should ease my mind or concern the hell out of me. I go with concern. "Listen, you don't know my father, but I can tell you he won't pay a ransom." It is the truth and a fact that has been drummed into me since I was a little girl.

My kidnapper's eyes twinkle for a second as if I've amused him.

"You're going to have to let me go," I say, reaching behind my back for a door handle.

"That door doesn't open," the driver says, sounding bored, even though he's driving so fast the buildings on either side of the rainy night meld together.

I look again at the man who carried me so easily away from danger. "Did you hire the men shooting at Duke?" I rear up.

"They were shooting at you, beautiful," he says, losing the amusement.

"Well, they weren't very good shots," I mutter, looking for any sort of escape.

He settles his massive shoulders against his seat. "You might as well relax because we have a bit of a drive in front of us."

I focus on the scruff covering his jaw—his very angled, cut, and masculine jaw.

All of a sudden, the driver yanks a phone to his ear and starts barking orders in Irish Gaelic. Something about three ports of entry and taking control of shipments.

My captor lifts his phone to his ear, his voice a low rumble that licks across my skin. What the heck is wrong with me? Did I hit my head? Am I suffering from some sort of nervous system malfunction from nearly being split in two by a bullet?

Snapping out a bloodcurdling series of clear orders dealing with movement, timing, and sanctioned bloodshed, the dark haired fantasy next to me ends his call and slaps his phone against his muscular thigh. His hard, nicely defined, badass of a thigh.

Yep. Short-circuited. "Listen," I say softly, scrambling again for a lever to open my door. Based on what I decipher from the calls, the mammoth man is orchestrating strategic hits against shipments of his rivals. There isn't a doubt in my mind that he's in the Irish mafia, which does not bode well for me. At all. The one good thing is that they have no idea I speak Gaelic. "It's obvious you chaps are busy, so how about I take off now?"

He turns toward me, lifting his head slightly with his nostrils flaring, as if catching some kind of scent.

My ovaries roll over and jump up and down. Seriously. I'm losing my mind.

"Say something else," he orders. No man has ever looked at me like he's starving and I'm the perfect meal. Until now.

Air catches in my throat. I clear it. "Why?"

"Something sweet."

Okay. This is getting weirder.

"Damn it." The driver swerves, one hand still on the phone at his ear. "Thorn? We need to be at the port, damn it."

Thorn? As in Thorn Beathach? I gulp. "Um..."

"This is more important," Thorn growls. "The boys can handle the job."

My fear of the Irish mafia pales as reality slaps me upside the head. Hard. "You're Thorn Beathach?" I whisper, my heart clanging against my ribcage so fast my chest compresses. I hope I'm too young for a heart attack.

His lips slightly part. "Say my name again."

Oh, crap. There is a reason Beathach has stayed out of the public eye. He's nuts. Gorgeous...but crazy. "All righty, then." I can't find the door handle. "I seriously doubt your boys will succeed without you at the port, so how about you drop me off and go get your work done?" No doubt the job is illegal and I don't want to know anything more than what I just heard.

He breathes in as if he's breathing *me*.

His phone buzzes and he lifts it to his ear, instantly launching into a spate of Gaelic.

I have to get out of this situation before he wraps those humongous hands around my neck. If my door is locked, perhaps his is not. The guy is twice my size, if not more, and looks like solid head-to-toe muscle. But I know better than to let them take me to the woods or wherever they plan to kill me. So it's now or never. When he turns to look out the window at the darkened night and issues even more orders, I find my chance. Taking a deep breath, I launch my body across the seat, elbow him hard in the throat, and yank on his door handle. The door starts to open and my heart leaps into my throat at how fast the wet asphalt flies by. Doesn't matter. I have to jump.

Without seeming to move, Thorn manacles an arm across my

waist, dumps me around to sit on his hard-assed lap, and slams the door shut.

I jerk and look up, meeting the driver's gaze in the rearview mirror. "Fuck," he says, the note almost admiring.

Sitting perfectly still, I try to calm my breathing. My skirt has ridden up to my thighs, and the material is trapped beneath my rear, so I can't pull it down. Not only are Thorn's thighs hard, his entire body is warm. Hot, even. The heat seeps toward me, circling me, tantalizing me in a way that negates any calming.

He finished his call and places his phone on the armrest. "Look at me, princess."

I push against him, trying to retake my seat. His abs are rock hard and ripple beneath the T-shirt. His arm doesn't tighten but I can't move. Is he the terminator or what? The arm is solid steel. So I turn, my breath catching at the raw heat in his eyes. "Let me go."

"No." His gaze drops to my lips, and they swell. Or at least, they feel like they swell with a shocking tingle. None of this makes sense. He continues in that devastatingly deep and now dominant tone. "I hadn't planned on establishing your rules until we arrive, but apparently I need to do so now."

Rules? My head jerks and I plant a hand on his chest. "I don't do rules, buddy."

He licks his bottom lip and lets out a soft hum. "You do now."

"Where are we going?" I ask, my butt feeling soft against his legs.

"My place."

I blinked. "You're going to kill me at your house?" I lean in, studying his eyes. Clear pupils, no sign of being on drugs. "You know it's a mistake, right?"

One of his dark eyebrows rises. "Do tell."

My brain finally just explodes and I start to babble. "You know, DNA evidence. Blood, saliva, tears, and all of that. If you're going to murder somebody, you want to do it far away from your house.

Also, leave the murder weapon." Though, looking at him, I know he *is* the murder weapon.

He cocks his head and a glimmer twinkles in his eyes.

I take that as encouragement. "Right? So now that you know that fact, you should plan better. How about you let me off here, and I'll meet you near the Golden Gate bridge next Saturday night? That way, there's no way to connect us." I know it's stupid to hope that he's *that* crazy, but it's all I have going for me right now.

"You promise you'll be there?" he asks.

I brighten. "Absolutely."

His free hand settles across my throat, his long fingers wrapping all the way around to my nape. His massive paw is heavy and heated, and there is no doubt he can snap my neck in a second if he chooses.

I jolt, swallowing and then finding relief that I *can* swallow.

He leans in and slightly squeezes. "That makes two rules of mine you've broken within ten minutes, Alana Beaumont. You break another one before we get home, and I'm going to flip you over and spank that perfect ass until you're screaming."

So he does know exactly who I am. The threat, from another man, would infuriate me until I drew blood. But this one? His hard and oddly possessive tone slams right to my core, zinging heat and fire so fast I nearly groan. Maybe insanity is contagious. "What do you want from me?"

"At the moment? Obedience." He glances at his buzzing phone.

"Bummer," I blather.

His gaze returns to me. "Excuse me?"

"There's a gene that leads to obedience," I say wisely, my head spinning. He's holding me too tightly for me to grasp the door handle again, so I need to loosen his grip. "Researchers have identified it on the Y chromosome, which I do not have." I test the waters and try to push away from him...but don't move an inch.

Man, he's strong. "But the good news is that learning to live with disappointment builds character. So you should be a decent guy in about a millennia with several more disappointments like this. I'm grateful to have started you on this journey."

His stare deepens and I want to blink but can't look away. "You're humorous. I had not expected that."

A tremble slakes through me. Somehow, I channel my inner Wonder Woman and tear my gaze from his, looking down at his broad chest. "You have enough going on, Thorn. You don't want to start a war with my father."

"I'm already in a war. Having another adversary doesn't change the chess board much," he counters. "You broke my rule by lying about meeting me."

"What other rule did I break?"

He loosens his hold on my neck and swipes a calloused thumb along my jawline. "We're traveling at about a hundred miles an hour, and you tried to jump out of the vehicle. Rule number two is to stay out of danger. Period."

"You're all danger," I say without thinking.

His grin is quick and gone so quickly I'd wonder if I saw it if my nipples didn't sharpen instantly. "Smart girl."

Obviously he doesn't truly think that, and I'm fine with letting him have his delusions for now. I decide to test his rules. "Why are you kidnapping me?"

"Rescuing you," he says. "The men in the bar were hired to take you. Maybe kill you, but I don't know the mission perimeters yet."

"Who hired them?" I ask, straightening as the blood beat faster between my ears.

He looks at the driver who shakes his head. "We don't know yet. They're a part of a vigilante group we keep an eye on, and they're open to any contracts. I will find out who hired them, I promise you."

Why would anybody want me dead? That is, if I believe him. "Perhaps your sources suck."

He blinks. Just once. Ah. The big bad, Irish billionaire badass isn't used to people doubting his word? I open my eyes wide like the bonehead he thinks me to be.

His gaze narrows. "I assure you my sources are excellent."

I lift a shoulder. "How do you know? I mean, if they suck, you wouldn't know it, would you?"

It sounds like a chuckle comes from the front seat, but when I glance at the driver, he's intently focused on the dark road in front of us.

"I would like to get off your lap now," I say primly.

Thorn studies me for a moment. "Pity." Then he releases his hold, lifts me, and settles me safely back in my seat.

Coldness sweeps along me and I miss his heat as I yank the flimsy skirt down as far as possible, which isn't very damn far. "Thank you for the rescue. Now you may take me home." I have never been manhandled before, and I'm over this. All of it.

"No."

"Why?" I tilt my head. He doesn't need money, and he's already at war. "Why take on my family?"

He eyes actually burn through the darkness. "Your family and those of your intended failed to keep you safe tonight. I did. Until I destroy who's trying to kill you, Beautiful, I'm keeping you safe." He lowers his chin. "Besides. Your family has absolutely no idea where you are. Nobody does."

Holiday Rogue

Chapter One

A dog blocked the entrance to her apartment.

Not just a dog, but a massive mutt that stretched across the entirety of the doorway, lying on his belly, his nose on his paws. Slowly, he lifted his head to study her, his eyes a deep brown against the multitude of colors in the fur around his snout—black, brown, white...a commingling of hues that gave him an uneven look.

Dogs were cute. They were fluffy. This one looked dangerous.

Marlie faltered a few feet away, snow clinging to the tops of her boots, and then looked at the closed apartment doors on either side of her. The converted turn-of-the-century house held three apartments, and hers was at the far end. Guarded by a dog so ugly, he was adorable.

He yawned and flashed sharp and deadly teeth.

She swallowed and took a step back. This was so weird. How had he gotten into the house? She'd had to unlock the front door to even make it inside to the hallway. "Um, hello?"

The dog blinked.

She once again looked at the closed doors on either side of her and reached out to knock gently on the one to the right, not wanting to startle the beast. No sound came from within, so she moved to the other side of the hallway and knocked, keeping her gaze squarely on the animal. He seemed mellow enough, but he had to weigh around a hundred pounds and had seriously sharp teeth. No answer came from the second apartment, either.

Breathing in, she slowly exhaled. "Um. All right. Okay." She moved forward a couple of steps to see if he reacted. He didn't. "So, um, you're in front of my door." She kept her voice gentle and non-threatening.

His left ear twitched.

"I've never had a dog, but we've had cats and fish through the years." She took several steps closer. "I need to get inside, and you're in the way. So, if it's okay, how about I gently reach over you and unlock my door?" Fishing her key out of her bag, she held her breath and unlocked it, pushing it open. "Good boy," she murmured. "Or girl. My guess is boy." She caught her breath. "I'm going to step over you—"

The dog stretched to his impressive height, turned, and sauntered right into her apartment.

"Oh." She bit her lip. What if he had to go to the bathroom? "Do you need to go outside?"

He scouted the boxes set neatly against the far wall of the living room, his tail wagging.

"I don't have furniture yet." She moved in behind him, keeping the door open. Should she call the dogcatcher? The animal looked healthy and well-kept. Certainly, he had a family. "I just can't figure out why you're here. *How* you got here."

He ignored her and continued sniffing through her boxes.

The outside door opened, and Marlie turned, her breath catching as a man loped inside the building. The winter sun poured in behind him, shrouding his face, but he filled out the space nicely with hard-packed muscle.

He paused. "Fabio?" His voice was a low rumble that slid right over her skin.

The dog barked once and bounded out, heading toward the man at full speed. The guy crouched and took the full impact of the hit, wrapping his sinewed arms around the animal and chuckling. "I missed you, too." He vigorously scrubbed both hands through the dog's fur and then stood, moving toward her.

She instinctively stepped back and then stopped herself.

"Hi." This close, his features took shape, and...man, what features he had. His hair was a shaggy light brown, his eyes a golden brown, and several cuts and scrapes looked at home on his angular features. It looked like he hadn't shaved in a few days. He wore an olive-colored shirt and camouflage pants with matching boots, all of which stretched nicely across a body honed for muscle and strength. A battered hat with an Air Force emblem on it covered the mass of hair.

"Hi." She swallowed and looked down at the happily panting dog butting against his leg. "Fabio?"

"Yeah." The guy held out a hand. "Sorry about that. My brother was going out of town for the week and dropped him off an hour earlier than he was supposed to so we could hang. Usually, Fabio just waits at my door. But he likes people, and he loves mysteries." He angled his head to see past her to her rows of boxes.

She faltered and then accepted his callused hand. "Oh." Warmth instantly slid up her arm.

"Bosco Albertini. Happy Monday, and it's nice to meet you." That intense gaze shot right into her eyes, and all sorts of feelings headed south.

Bosco? Very cool name. "Marlie Kreuk. Your new neighbor." Should she invite him in? Why? It wasn't like she had a place for him to sit. "I didn't know we could have pets in the building."

He released her and flashed a charming grin with an intriguing edge. "We can't. Fab isn't my dog, but he stays with me sometimes when my brother is out on a job. We keep it a secret around here."

"No problem." She smiled at the happily panting mutt. "He's adorable."

Bosco chuckled. "Well, he's something. Mrs. Balerto, who used to live in your apartment, snuck him doggy treats. She moved with her niece to Florida, and Fabio hasn't gotten the message yet. He was probably looking for yummies."

Marlie pressed a hand to the doorframe. "I'll have to keep that in mind." Then her gaze ran over the cuts and bruises on his face. "Rough mission?"

"Normal mission with an extra side of training thrown in." He wiped a scab near his chin, emotionally withdrawing without moving a muscle. "I'd invite you in for food or something as a welcome to the building, but I haven't been home in two months, and there's nothing in the fridge." His hand dropped to pet the dog's head. "My place is probably full of dust and discarded mail, anyway."

She smiled. "That's okay. Fabio was a lovely welcome to the building, and it was very nice to meet you." She wanted to start unpacking and stop looking at the too-hot guy who'd just become her neighbor.

Bosco nodded. "Yeah. Welcome to Timber City, Marlie." He turned and headed toward his apartment with the dog dancing around his feet.

She swallowed and shut her door. Wow. She had just moved to town and definitely wasn't looking for romance. But even so. That was one fine male body. Sighing, she turned to unpack. It was time to get organized, and she'd do it without thinking about her sexy neighbor. Yeah, right.

As darkness started to fall, Bosco carried bins of Christmas decorations to his door, narrowly escaping tripping over the dog. "Would you please get out of the way?" He chuckled. "I should've left you at Nonna's house." He opened his door, stepped inside, and set the containers safely against the wall. The entire apartment smelled musty and deserted. He kicked his boots out of the way, and even though he'd wiped off the snow at the entrance to the house, more still scattered on the wood.

A small cry had his head shooting up.

Fabio barked and ran into the hall, dashing so hard toward Marlie's door that he hit it head-on.

Bosco followed, automatically scanning for any threats. He knocked, edging sideways in case he needed to break down the door. "Marlie?"

The door opened, and she stood there, blowing hair out of her face. A dollop of dust smudged her smooth cheek, and her wild hair gave her a just-kissed look. "Hi. Sorry. I slipped on the counter."

His eyebrows rose. "Why were you on the counter?"

"The top cupboards are high up there," she said, her smile simply adorable.

His body warmed. The woman was about five-two with sandy-blond hair, stunning hazel eyes, and feline features. "I'm often used by family and friends to fetch things from a top shelf. I can help, if you want." Then the scent of something freakin' delicious caught his attention, and he lifted his head to sniff. "What is that?"

She opened the door and gestured him inside a mess of boxes, crumpled packing paper, and garbage bags. "Comfort food. Cheesy noodle casserole along with sugar cookies with chocolate in the middle. Are you hungry?"

"Yes." He shouldn't be, considering Nonna had just fed him. But with the delicious aroma, he could probably eat again. "Tell you what? Why don't I put everything on the top shelves that you want there, and you can pay me in food?" It was a fair trade.

"Okay." She leaned down and petted Fabio.

Bosco shut the door and headed into her kitchen. He was familiar with the apartment because Mrs. Balerto had pretty much adopted him as a grandson, which meant a lot of homemade food. The living room was quaint with a white-painted mantel over the

5

fireplace, the kitchen updated with stainless steel appliances, and a cute powder room by the door. He'd never been in Mrs. B's bedroom or master bath.

"I just need those other two dishes up on the top shelves. I don't use them." Marlie pointed to some fragile-looking white bowls. She'd gotten a lot done during the day after their first meeting, and empty boxes littered the wall near the door.

He gently lifted the China to the top shelf and pushed them back a little. "There you go." Without waiting, he reached for a cookie and chewed happily. He looked around. "Do you have furniture coming?"

She nodded. "Yeah. My bedroom set arrived today, and everything else is supposed to come tomorrow." Then she dug into a grocery bag and drew out paper plates and utensils, looking around for something. "You know what? I forgot to buy drinks. Why did I forget that? All I have is water."

"I have beer," he said, scratching his head and trying to ignore how adorable she looked with her eyes all befuddled. Stunning green-and-brown eyes—the perfect shade of hazel. Nope. Not going there. He wasn't looking for a woman, and even if he were, it wouldn't be the one living next door to him. Not with his life and considering he might get transferred to do what he needed to do. "I'll go get the beer." At the moment, he could really use one. He hustled toward the door and out to the hallway.

Fabio didn't follow him.

He strode sedately into his apartment, grabbed the six-pack of beer, and fetched a bottle of red wine from the bin of decorations. Then he blew off the dust and moved back to her apartment. "Hey. I have a bottle of red from my nonna. She sent me home with Christmas decorations and wine this afternoon." He placed the Cabernet on the counter and dug his multi-purpose knife out of his back pocket. "I have an opener."

"I have glasses." She reached into the cupboard and drew down two wine goblets. "Where does your nonna live?"

"She lives over in Silverville by the river. It's a small mining town just through the pass." He opened the bottle. "My whole family either lives in Silverville or here in Timber City." He poured the wine.

She accepted a glass. "I wasn't aware there was an Air Force base in northern Idaho."

He grinned. "No. I'm stationed out of Fairchild on the other side of Spokane. I'm a pilot and work in air refueling support and hot-pit refueling." He opened a beer. "As well as a couple other specialties we don't need to talk about."

"Hot-pit refueling?" she asked.

"The jet lands, keeps one engine running, and you refuel it right then and there so it can head off again." He grinned, and his phone buzzed. He glanced down at the screen and then answered. "Hey, Rory. What's up?" It was good that Rory had called. Things were getting a little cozy, and he needed to get a grip.

"Hi. We're down at the Clumsy Penguin throwing darts. Get down here. I need a partner," Rory said, boisterous laughter behind him.

They'd just spent an entire weekend snowmobiling and camping in the freakin' snow since Bosco had returned—he hadn't even unpacked yet. "Yeah, okay. I'll be there in an hour." He clicked off and studied the pretty woman. "My brother and a bunch of buddies are partying down at a bar near the water. Want to see a little of the area?"

She blinked. "Ah, well."

He laughed. "I'm not asking you out, Marlie. Just seeing if you want to meet some folks and see a nice local bar."

"Why aren't you asking me out?" She tilted her head to the side, studying him.

The directness threw him. "I don't date. Not with my job and not right now—and I learned that the hard way." His schedule was hectic and last-minute oftentimes, and a woman deserved more than that from him. Another lesson he'd learned the hard way. He

7

scrubbed a hand through his shaggy hair, which was still a little damp from his shower earlier. "I'm all-in with friends with benefits, though." Nonna would so kick his ass for saying that, but he had to be honest.

A fine pink blush wandered across Marlie's pretty face. "I appreciate the honesty. So, yes, I'd like to meet some people and check out a local bar. No, I don't want to be friends with benefits. Finally, yes, I'd like to be friends." She looked at the cooling casserole. "Do we have time to eat first?"

"Definitely." His chest ached just enough to tick him off. His instincts, so sharply honed in the field, whispered that he was a moron. "I'll grab napkins."

Chapter Two

The Clumsy Penguin was a dive bar on a twisty lake road with worn wood, uneven floors, and wide windows overlooking the freezing-cold water. Christmas lights sparkled around every window while hard rock played through the speakers. It was, in a word, perfect—and surprisingly busy for a Monday night.

Marlie aimed a dart and threw, hitting the second ring of a seven.

"You're getting better," Bosco said, topping off her beer mug. The huge, thick, real glass kind still frozen from the freezer.

"Maybe." She sat on a black bar stool and leaned against the wall. "I haven't hit anything I've aimed at once, but I'm having fun." She'd never really spent much time playing darts.

A cute blond guy, probably in his early thirties, winked at her from near the bar. She smiled.

Bosco cut him a look, and the blond glanced away.

"We're just friends," Marlie muttered. "Remember?"

Bosco handed her another dart.

Rory lifted a round table from across the bar and carried it easily through a throng of partygoers to place it near them. He was as tall as Bosco with lighter brown hair, pure blue eyes, and as much scruff on his face as Bosco. There was no doubt they were brothers. The Albertini family had some seriously hot and rugged genes. "I ordered wings and potato skins," he said, depositing the table.

Marlie grinned and looked across the room. "Was anybody else using that table?" There were still two half-full beer glasses on it.

"Yeah, but I saved one of their asses when they got caught on a mountain last week. I work with search and rescue when I'm home." Rory shrugged. "Plus, food trumps beer. They can hold their beers if they come find them."

Bosco rolled his eyes and threw a dart, getting another bull's-eye. "I just got back to town and am not getting in a bar fight." He looked over his shoulder, scouting the room as if looking for threats.

Why did Marlie get the feeling she hadn't heard his entire pedigree when it came to his job? Not that it was any of her business.

Rory lifted his phone to his ear. "Quint? Get over the pass for the night. Bos is home, and we're playing." He shook his head. "Fine. Old man." He ended the call.

Bosco barked out a laugh. "You did not just call Quint old. Remember when he dug us both out of an avalanche with his bare hands? He was what? Fifteen?"

Rory grinned, showing what most definitely should be termed the Albertini dimple in his left cheek. Bosco had one, as well. "Yeah, but he's all domesticated now. The family bet is that he'll propose on Valentine's Day and get married in June."

Bosco sobered. "Quint hasn't had the best luck with women."

Rory waved him off. "He does now. Seriously. Her name is Heather, and you're going to freakin' love her. She's a sweetheart, and she adores him."

"Is he going to retire from the forest service and do something else, then?" Bosco asked, his brow still furrowed.

Marlie leaned forward. Being an only child, this interaction between brothers was fascinating.

"No." Rory waved toward the waitress, who immediately brought over another pitcher of beer before scooting down to pick up empties from another table. "She's totally fine with his job and doesn't want him to change for her. I'm tellin' you, he hit the mother lode. And while she's going to be our sister soon, I think it's okay to say right now that she's hot as fuck. Totally curvy."

"It is not okay to say that your future sister-in-law is hot as fuck." Bosco snorted. "You're such an ass."

"Doesn't make me wrong," Rory drawled.

Marlie took another sip of beer. "How many brothers do you have?"

"There are six of us," Rory said easily. "Bosco is the baby."

Bosco hip-checked his brother. "By one year. Seriously."

"I'm much more mature," Rory said, dragging over another black-topped stool. "So, you haven't said. What brought you to Timber City, Marlie?"

"A job at the college," she replied, taking another drink and enjoying the slide from hard rock to Christmas music. "I teach Chinese, and there was an opening with a tenure track."

Bosco handed her a dart. "Very cool. Why Chinese?"

This close, he smelled like the outdoors. "My mom was from Indonesia, and I grew up speaking several languages. Have a knack for them." The food arrived, and her stomach growled.

"What about Italian?" Rory drawled.

She nodded. "My grandmother on my dad's side was Italian, so it was one of the languages I wanted to learn. I may teach the Intro to Italian class at the college, as well."

Bosco hissed in a breath. "Not a word, Rory," he muttered.

Rory barely kept the amusement out of his eyes as he handed out small and cracked plates. "Where did you move from?"

"Seattle. I taught at a school there but was ready to get out of the city." She dug into the chicken wings, feeling comfortable and accepted by these guys. Country boys and tough guys, who were happy that their older brother was in love. "Why would Quint have to change his job working as a forester?"

Bosco grinned and finished a chicken wing. "He's a smoke jumper for the forest service."

Apparently, the Albertini boys were all adrenaline junkies. "Okay. Let me get this straight, Bosco. You work for the military, Rory works for search and rescue, and Quint jumps into fires. What about the other three brothers?" An unusual longing for a big family hit her. Her parents had both passed away in a car accident, and she hadn't had any other family.

Bosco nudged the potato skins toward her. "Vince was honorably discharged from the Marines after being shot too many times and now owns and runs an outfitting company on the river. Finn and Knox are co-owners, also ex-military, and have a couple of other businesses. And, for the record, search and rescue is Rory's hobby. His job is a big ol' secret."

Rory tossed a napkin at his brother.

Marlie chuckled. "Excuse me, boys." She set her beer down and wound her way through the crowd to the restroom, where she stood in line and then took care of business. She walked back out into the heat and noise, surprised when somebody grasped her arm. She turned and then relaxed and smiled. "Mark Jones."

"Hi." The young professor stood near the bar, looking handsome in dark jeans and a thick sweater. He taught philosophy at the college, and they'd met during orientation since they were both new at the school. "I see you found the local hangout for winter fun."

She nodded. "Yeah. This place is wonderful."

"Me, too." He nodded toward three guys playing pool. "Bob and Joe teach in the mathematics department, and Frank is in HR at the college. Would you like to join us for a game or two?" His eyes were an intriguing light blue, his shoulders wide, and there was no doubt he was smart.

"I would, but I'm here with friends." She noticed the interest in his gaze, and while he was cute, she didn't need to get involved with anybody from the school. At least not before she even started work. Her gaze caught on his ring finger, which held a white line she hadn't noticed before.

He sighed. "I moved here because of my divorce. Was married for three years. She left me for a guy she worked with." He scrubbed a hand through his thick black hair. "I wish this stupid line would fade."

Marlie smiled, feeling for the guy. "Maybe go to a tanning booth and tan your whole hand." She patted his arm. "A fresh start is a good thing." The skin at the base of her neck prickled, and she turned to see Bosco leaning against the far wall next to his brother, watching them. Well, watching *her*. His gaze was unreadable, but her heartbeat kicked right into gear anyway.

Mark followed her gaze. "Oh, crap. I'm sorry. I didn't realize you were on a date."

"I'm not," she said, turning her attention back to him. "These guys are just my friends, but they seem the alert type. I'll see you at the school."

"I'm looking forward to it." Mark proved he hadn't lost the ability to flirt after his divorce.

She chuckled and turned to wind through bodies to reach the Albertini men.

"Meet a friend?" Bosco asked mildly.

"Yeah," she said, reaching for her beer and hopping up onto a stool. "Mark is a fellow professor at the college." Not that it was any of Bosco's business. The guy was kind of sending her mixed messages, and she wasn't into playing games. "Why do you ask, Bosco?"

He sighed. "Just making sure you're safe. You're new in town, and I hadn't realized you'd already met people."

Rory snorted and then reached for the darts. "Are we ready for another game? I can throw left-handed this time."

Bosco hip-butted him. "I won last time, jackass. How about

we play for something interesting? Say that new snowmobile you just bought. It's a beauty."

"Not in a million," Rory said easily, grinning and looking around. Then he sobered. "Jennie is here."

Bosco's smile remained in place, but his eyes hardened and then veiled. "I guess I should go say hello. Is anybody with her?"

Rory's gaze didn't seem to move from Bosco's face. "A couple of girlfriends. You don't need to go say hi. Let her come to you."

Marlie's heart rate picked up. She shifted uneasily on her chair. Was this why Bosco had been all *friends with benefits* with her? She partially turned to see three women walking inside, all wearing heavy coats covered in snow.

Bosco leaned toward her. "Would you excuse me for a minute?"

She turned and looked him right in the eye. "Why wouldn't I?" They weren't on a date.

His pupils narrowed in a way that made her lungs feel funny. Or maybe that sensation slid a little south of her lungs. "Agreed, but I did bring you here, and that makes you my responsibility."

Sweet and old-fashioned...and just a friend—no matter how quickly her nipples had just hardened. She leaned in, appreciating the further narrowing of his eyes. "I'm a big girl and more than capable of taking care of myself, Bosco Albertini. However..." She let her voice soften. "If I ever need somebody to guard my chastity, I know just where to find you."

Rory burst out laughing but quickly recovered by coughing and taking a big swig of beer.

"You're a moron," Bosco muttered to him. "I'll be right back." He turned and walked away.

Chapter Three

B osco wound through the bar, keeping a bead on the blond chugging tequila like sugar water. The guy had winked at Marlie more than once, and he was rapidly becoming stupid drunk if his rising decibels were any indication.

Then, he reached Jennie. "Hi."

She blinked, her eyes widening. They were a clear green that contrasted nicely with her dark blond hair. "Hi. I didn't know you were home on leave." She sounded apologetic.

Her two friends shifted uneasily.

He looked at them. "Hi, Mandy. Hi, Louise. It's good to see you two."

It was the right tone because they both visibly relaxed. "Hi," they said in unison.

He forced a smile, taking note that he no longer felt as if he'd been kicked in the balls when he stood this close to Jennie. "Anyway, I saw you here and wanted to just say hi and that I hope everything is going well."

She blushed and unzipped her coat. "It is. Work is great, and we've been really busy with so many clients." She worked as a physical therapist in a small clinic on the Idaho and Washington border and was good at her job. "Um, how about you?"

He helped her with the coat and hung it on one of the myriad free hooks near the door. "I'm good."

Her gaze ate up his face, narrowing at the cuts near his eye. "Looks like air refueling of planes is as dangerous as ever."

That was one of their problems. He could never give her the whole truth about his job, although he *was* an expert in air refueling. "Yeah, well, we all know how dangerous a paper cut can be."

She laughed, as he'd meant her to.

Then he patted her arm. "Anyway, it's good to see you. I have to get back to Rory. He thinks he's the king of darts." He turned and bit back the reminder that the roads were icy and to be careful. She wasn't his to worry about any longer.

Then he made his way through the throng to reach his brother, who was making Marlie laugh with a story about Knox when he'd come home with Fabio.

"You good?" Rory asked, his stance still casual.

"Yep." Bosco reached for his beer, surprise filtering through him that it was the truth.

Marlie swung a jean-clad leg from the barstool. "How long ago did you guys break up?"

He turned to her, his eyebrows rising. "Six months ago."

Her leg kept swinging. "Because of your job?"

Smart little thing, wasn't she? He nodded. "Yeah."

She pursed her lips. "Nobody ever dumped me because of my job," she mused, her eyes a little cloudy from the beer. "Although, one guy did because I kept beating him at chess."

Rory snorted. "True story?"

She nodded sadly.

Bosco smiled, feeling the amusement and grateful for it. "No kidding? Did you think of letting him win?"

"Yeah," she murmured. "But then I'd be dating a guy I'd have to let win at silly games. And, really, what fun is that?"

"Totally agree," Bosco murmured, taking a deep drink of his beer. The woman was becoming more and more likable, and the blond guy at the bar was getting more and more ballsy. The guy lifted his drink in her direction in cheers.

To her credit, she pretended she didn't see him. "Oh, and another man dumped me because I didn't want to engage in puppy play." She shivered. "I make no judgments about kink and what people want but wearing a tail just couldn't be my thing."

Humor attacked Bosco so hard he coughed out beer, laughing along with Rory.

Rory caught his breath first, wiping off his chin. "Please tell me you're joking."

She shook her head and wobbled a little on the stool. "Nope. True story. When he said he wanted to show me his special leash, I was out of there. It was only our second date, for goodness sakes."

Bosco was laughing so hard he thought he might lose a kidney.

He looked around and caught sight of Jennie, who was staring at Marlie.

Rory reached for another chicken wing. "You're funny, Marlie. I'm glad Bosco found you."

She sipped more beer, her hair sliding over her narrow shoulders. "Actually, Fabio found me. Bosco has made it more than clear that we're just friends." She held out her glass, her hand wobbling a little. "Friends are awesome. To friends." Bosco and Rory both clinked with her, and Rory gave him a look that clearly called him a moron.

Bosco looked right back. It wasn't as if Mr. CIA was looking for a woman right now, either. Yet, in the darkened tavern, with Christmas lights twinkling all around and showing the green in Marlie's intelligent eyes, he stepped a bit closer to her. Just a little bit.

Of course, the blond chose that moment to make his move. He pushed his way through the crowd toward her. "Hi."

She blinked and gingerly set her glass on the table. "No."

The guy paused. "Huh?"

"'No." She smiled, still kicking her feet. "I'm surrounded by as much testosterone as I need right now, as you can see. Thank you for saying hi and for winking at me from across the bar because that was fun. You're cool, and that's nice. So, hi and have a good night."

The guy cocked his head, seeming to think about her statement before looking at Rory and finally at Bosco. Then, miracles of all miracles, he grew a brain. "Cool. All right. Have a good night." He sidled around Bosco and returned to the bar.

Marlie smiled widely. "Isn't it nice when no punches have to be thrown?"

"It really is," Bosco said, eyeing her from over the top of his glass. Putting her in the friend zone was the right thing to do.

Probably.

BOSCO ROLLED HIS NECK, his left leg aching as he stomped through the snow and up the stairs of the house. He kicked snow off his boots, noting that the owner of the rental house and apartments had set up a couple of glowing Santas in the front yard. He moved inside and hitched to his door, just as Marlie's opened.

"Hey," she said, her smile pretty.

"Hey." He leaned against his door, wishing she wasn't so appealing. But she was, and that was a stupid thing to wish for, anyway. "What's up?"

She drew out a large roll of red and green wrapping paper. "I was going to decorate my door. I have tons of this stuff." She looked down at the huge roll. "Want me to do yours, too?"

He grinned. "No, but thanks." Then he winced.

Her eyebrow arched. "Are you okay?"

"Yeah. Hand-to-hand training today. It was all good." He partially turned as the outside door opened.

Rory stalked inside with a bouncing Fabio at his feet. "I have orders to leave first thing in the morning. Fabio is yours until Knox gets home." He paused. "Oh. Hi, Marlie. Nice holiday roll."

She chuckled. "Thanks."

Bosco shook his head. "I'm shipping out first thing, too. I can't take the dog."

Marlie's eyebrows lifted. "You're both leaving?" She shuffled her feet, looking a bit lonely. "Well, how about you come in for a goodbye dinner? I made a huge chicken casserole. You're more than invited."

Rory was already moving beyond Bosco to reach Marlie's door. "Sure. That's great. Thanks. I'll help you with the wrapping paper. Whole door?"

"Yeah." She looked at the happily panting dog. "I could watch him for a while if you want."

Bosco shook his head. "Thanks, but I've got it." It wasn't fair of them to take advantage of her sweet nature. Well, except to eat dinner. He was starving. So, he motioned for the dog to follow, and they all tromped into her apartment. He whistled. "Nice."

"Thanks." Her furniture was a comfortable and thick white sofa with matching chairs, and a large Christmas tree already twinkled from the corner by the fireplace. The woman had moved in fully, now, hadn't she?

Fabio ran over and flattened himself in front of the gas fireplace, which crackled merrily—or at least blew merrily.

Rory made quick work of the door, and soon, all three of them were eating the delicious chicken casserole. Bosco cast Marlie several looks, but the woman truly seemed to just enjoy their company. Oh, he'd told women before that he wasn't looking for romance, and they'd still flirted or tried to get him to change his mind.

Not Marlie. She seemed perfectly content with how things were.

Should that bother him? Because it freaking did.

Rory finished eating. "Man, that was good." He grinned. "I like to cook, but it isn't a skill. My girl can't cook, either. She almost burned down an entire campground while making mac and cheese."

"Your girl?" Marlie asked, her eyes lighting up. "You're married?"'

"Nope," Rory said. "Serenity and I were engaged for about two months, and then she threw the ring at my head. But we'll get back together soon."

Bosco sighed. "It's been three months, bro. You're not getting back together."

Marlie's expression softened, making her pretty eyes look more tawny than green in the evening light. "I'm so sorry."

Rory's jaw tightened, and his eyes held that glow that probably scared terrorists or whoever he dealt with when he was away from home. "There's nothing to be sorry about. We had a misunderstanding, and I'm giving her time and space to figure things out." He glanced at his watch. "We're a few weeks out from the new year, and that's her deadline to do so."

Marlie cut Bosco a look and then focused on his brother. "Um, what then?"

"Then she's out of time and space," Rory said evenly. "I'll help her figure the rest out."

Shit. His brother really would kidnap Serenity if she didn't get her act together. But she was stubborn and smart--and right now really pissed. Bosco shook his head. "Dude. You lied to her." The poor woman had thought Rory worked for the forest service like Quint, except he traveled more to federal lands.

"I did not lie," Rory retorted. "I can't talk about my work, and you know it."

Yeah, and he also knew that Serenity McDerny was a stubborn-ass Irishwoman. "Don't come to me for stitches when she shoots off your balls." Bosco stood and cleared his plate, not liking how familiar he felt. Marlie looked kissable, plain and simple, and he had to pull his head out of his ass and stop thinking about her sweet mouth.

He had his rules for a reason. Yeah. Jennie. That had been a painful lesson and one he wasn't going to repeat—especially with a kind hearted woman like Marlie. "Can I use your—?"

She nodded. "Yeah. To the left of my office."

He headed to the bathroom as Marlie and Rory finished clearing the dishes, noting the cheerful reindeer candles in the small powder room. She sure liked to decorate for the holidays. He walked out, catching the tail end of a conversation that was none of his business.

"You two make a nice couple," Rory was saying. "Why don't you ask Bos out?"

Marlie laughed, the sound soft. "He made it very clear the first day we met that we were in full friend zone."

Rory clinked a dish, no doubt washing with too much soap like usual. His brother was like a hound dog on a scent, and for some reason, the tough guy had always been a matchmaker. "Yeah, but you could change his mind."

"Nope." She turned off the water. "I deal in reality, and we're in the friend zone. That's all there is."

Bosco paused, wondering if he'd lost his way. The strong urge to change his mind, to change *hers*, smashed into his gut like an iron ball. For now, he had to find somebody to watch the dog so he could get to work a long way from home—or rather in the air a long way from home. Then he'd figure out what to do with his too-beautiful neighbor.

Chapter Four

Marlie locked her apartment door and double-checked that she'd remembered her shopping list. Yep. All right. She really couldn't forget the flour again. She strode past Bosco's door and paused when the sound of barking came from inside. What the heck? After dinner the night before, Bosco had said that he'd be on the road at dawn, and it was much later than that. He hadn't left the dog all alone, waiting for somebody to pick him up, had he?

She bit her lip and gingerly knocked on the door.

It opened, and a stunning woman stood there in boxer shorts, a ripped T-shirt, and bare feet. She had her brownish-red hair piled on her head in a messy bun, and her grayish-green eyes were bleary. She rubbed one. "Morning?"

Marlie took a step back. What in the world? What kind of games did Bosco play? This was nuts. "Sorry, I—"

Fabio shoved by the woman and nearly ran Marlie over, panting happily.

She patted his head. "I heard him bark and thought he was alone, but that didn't make sense." She started backing away, but the dog made it nearly impossible by winding around her legs.

"I'm sorry to have disturbed your sleep." The woman really was beautiful without makeup.

"Fabio. Inside, now," the woman said, snapping her fingers.

The dog obeyed instantly, heading back inside.

"Wow. He doesn't usually listen from what I've seen," Marlie mused.

The woman's eyes cleared and then focused. "Oh. You're Marlie." She smiled, flashing a dimple.

"I am. Yes." Marlie shook her head, trying to get her bearings. This was just weird. "I—"

"I'm Anna." She held out a hand. "Albertini. Anna Albertini, Bosco's cousin. Rory told me you'd moved in next door." Her smile was friendly, and yep, there was the Albertini dimple again.

So, Rory and not Bosco had told Anna about Marlie. Yep. Just buddies for sure. For a minute the night before, she'd wondered if they could have something else, but then he'd shut down. "Hi." She shook Anna's hand. "I'm sorry if I woke you up."

"Oh, I've been up a few times with the dog and was just snoozing. It's been a rough week." Anna pushed her hair away from her face.

The front door to the house flew open, and a muscled man with seriously pissed blue eyes stomped down the hallway toward the three apartment doors. He was as big and muscled as Bosco and Rory. Was there something in the water in Idaho, or what?

"It's about to get worse," Anna murmured, watching the guy impassively.

Marlie took an instinctive step away.

"What the holy hell are you thinking, Angel?" the man snapped, an Irish brogue emerging with what had to be temper.

Anna didn't seem fazed by the guy's size or his anger. She yawned again. "Listen. I know things have been crazy, but I'm not giving up the case. My Glock is in my bag, I've remembered every move you've taught me, and I'm safe."

The Irish guy leaned in and down, his nose about an inch away from Anna's. "Your Glock had better be in your bag, you had better remember the training, and for all that's holy, you are not safe. In fact, I know you're not safe because your ass isn't at your sister's house where it should be right now."

The Irish dude was both a little scary and a lot sexy. By the light pink filtering across Anna's face, she might agree with that. She met the guy's glare evenly, not backing down a bit. "Aiden, I am not giving up this case."

"I'm not asking you to give it up," the guy snapped, his thick black hair looking as if he'd been yanking at it out of frustration. "What I *am* doing is asking you to be safe, and hightailing your very nice butt across town to babysit a dog is not doing that."

Anna rolled her eyes. "Bos was called out, and I said I'd watch Fabio until Knox got home, which is tonight. Nobody knows I'm here. So, stop bossing me around."

Apparently, it was the wrong thing to say. Anna was on her feet one second, and the next, she was over Aiden's shoulder, heading inside the apartment. "Damn it," she muttered, not seeming too perturbed. "Fabio, come!"

The dog happily bounced around them.

Anna levered up, balancing herself with a hand on the middle of Aiden's back. "Sorry about this, Marlie. It has to seem weird." She flopped back down.

Marlie remained frozen in place. Then she jerked herself out of it. "Hey. Are you okay? I could hit him from behind if you want." Then, without waiting for an answer, she ran ahead and jumped in front of Aiden, nearly tripping over the dog.

Anna laughed out loud.

Aiden sighed heavily. "That's sweet of you." Then he ducked and lifted an overnight bag over his free shoulder, tossed a hand-knitted blanket over Anna's form, and headed right back out into the hallway.

Marlie wavered and then followed, running in front of him

and blocking the outside door. She had no chance of beating him in a fight, but she could probably take out his knee. "Should I call in a kidnapping?"

Anna laughed harder, and Aiden kept coming straight at her, amusement tilting his full lips.

"I'm thinking the Albertini family might be a little odd," Marlie muttered.

That stopped Aiden cold. His eyes warmed, showing a conglomeration of blues. "They are. Get out now if you can. Trust me. Run fast and run far."

Anna laughed harder, squirming over his very broad shoulder, his hand on her thigh holding her in place.

Marlie swallowed. "We're just friends. I mean, Bosco and me. Just friends."

"Ha," Aiden said, sidestepping her easily. "That's how they get you, darlin'. I've already heard about you, which means the family has heard, and you're as good as in. I hope you like big weddings." He kept walking.

Anna whistled. "Fabio, come!"

The dog panted after them.

A phone rang from the big bag over Aiden's shoulder. He sighed, stopped again, and yanked it out to hand to Anna.

She pressed a speaker button as if she talked to people all the time while hanging over Aiden's very broad back. "Hey, Bosco," she answered easily. "I have the dog."

"What the fuck are you doing going to my apartment by yourself when dead bodies keep showing up around you?" Bosco yelled, his voice somehow low and pissed, even while yelling.

Marlie paused, catching her breath. Dead bodies? Seriously?

"Exactly," Aiden said.

Anna sighed. "Bosco—"

"No. I'm headed into a war zone, damn it. Devlin? Do you have this?" Bosco snapped.

"I'm about to," Aiden said agreeably.

"Good. I don't care what anybody says. You're a fucking saint." Bosco ended the call.

Marlie's insides went all jittery. *War zone?*

Aiden stalked toward the outside door again. "I am a saint," he muttered. "Should get a medal or something."

Anna levered up, placing her hand in the middle of Aiden's back again and lifting her head so her gaze could meet Marlie's. "Hey, Marlie. Lock up Bosco's apartment for me, would you? Thanks so much. I tell you what? I'll give you a call when this case is over, and we can grab a drink. What's your number?"

Marlie rattled it off as quickly as she could. The front door opened and then shut, taking them out into the snowy day.

Quiet descended.

Marlie reached for Bosco's door and shut it, locking it. Maybe it was a good thing—a really good thing—that she and Bosco were just friends. The Albertini family seemed absolutely crazy. Then she caught sight of Anna's wallet near the door, which had fallen out of the bag Aiden had thrown over his shoulder.

She grabbed it and ran outside just as he was loading Anna into the front seat of a black truck. "Your wallet," she breathed, handing it over.

A couple of cars sped past, throwing icy slush toward the truck. Marlie ducked, but spray covered her boots anyway.

"Thanks." Anna grinned. "Welcome to chaos, my new friend."

AFTER GRABBING a quick coffee where she'd been asked out on a date by a handsome accountant, Marlie headed to the college, parking outside her brick building and using her key to get inside. The college was quiet during the holiday season, and she hummed as she made her way up the stairs to the faculty offices. Hers was in the corner with windows overlooking the lake, and she smiled, feeling a sense of peace as the snow fell lightly over the water.

It took a few hours to get organized, and movement caught her attention outside her door. She looked up to see Mark carrying what looked like a couple of plants. His office was two doors down from hers, and he paused in the doorway. "Hey there."

She smiled. "Nice plants."

He snorted. "They're from my grandma. She sent them to my apartment, figuring I wouldn't find time to buy my own. Something about oxygen in the air helping me to think clearly." Today, he wore dark jeans, snow boots, and a thick black sweater that matched his hair. His intelligent eyes twinkled.

"She's probably right?" Marlie hadn't considered plants.

"Well, then." He moved inside the office and deposited one of the flowering bundles on her credenza. "Here's a welcome present. Since we're shaping young minds, I guess we should both have more oxygen in our offices." He peered at the foliage. "I'd love to tell you all about this plant and how much water it needs, but I have no idea. We'll have to google it."

She laughed. "Thanks for the present." She missed her friends from Seattle, and it was nice to be meeting people. She had a date with the guy from the coffee shop for lunch tomorrow and then for a night out this weekend, and that would help her stop spinning little fantasies about her too-sexy neighbor. Bosco had been gone for days, and she already worried about him.

Mark angled toward the door. "Do you want to grab lunch in an hour or so? There's a deli across the park that's supposed to be really good."

She swallowed. He was charming and good-looking, but she knew better than to date a colleague. Even so, what could lunch hurt? "Sure. I'll be finished with these files about then. We can walk across the park and check out the area." She'd been meaning to do so anyway.

His smile was wide. "Excellent." Then he disappeared down the hallway.

She winced. It wasn't a date. Her phone buzzed, and she answered it. "Hello."

"Hey, Sunshine. We miss you around here," Stacia, her friend who taught physics, said. "When are you coming home?"

Marlie kicked back in her chair and watched the snow falling outside. "I am home now. Why don't you come and visit me? You'd love the lake and the snow, and we could go skiing." Or, rather, go to the ski hill and drink hot toddies by the fireplace. Maybe take a run or two. "What do you say?"

"I say that sounds like fun," Stacia agreed. "I'm booked until after Christmas but could head over if the pass is open. Maybe the day after New Year's? We have that week off."

She sat up. "Really?" Excitement filtered through her. "It would be so great to see you. I'll find ski tickets and have the week planned." They'd been good friends for five years, and Marlie missed bouncing ideas off Stacia. "We'll have so much fun."

Stacia laughed. "We always do. For now, tell me about the local talent. Have you met anybody interesting?"

Marlie bit her lip and then told all, including her run-in with Bosco, the coffee-shop guy named Turner, and even Mark.

Stacia breathed out. "Seriously? Is there a shortage of women in Timber City, or what? I need to come visit just to find a date. What are you going to do about the neighbor?"

Marlie rolled her eyes. "I just told you that I have a date this weekend with a hottie and lunch today with another handsome man, and you're asking about Bosco? What's wrong with you?"

"Your voice changed when you talked about him," Stacia said wisely. "He's the one who interests you, even though you're in the friend zone. I mean, how could he not? Who is named Bosco Albertini? The name alone is beyond cool. Add in his job and the danger and those broad shoulders you described in way too much detail and, come on, I know you."

Marlie shook her head. "Nope. Not going there. You know when a guy warns you off that you should listen. Always."

"True." Stacia sighed. "Even so, I hope I get to meet him when I visit. Plus, it sounds like the Albertini family is a lot of fun."

Marlie chuckled. "I'm not sure *fun* is the right word. But they're definitely not boring."

Chapter Five

It had been a rough few days away from home, but it was Sunday, and Bosco was home and ready to relax. "Thanks for picking me up," he said to Rory, easing his aching body toward his doorway. He'd always trained hard in hand-to-hand, just in case a mission went wrong, and he ended up on the ground fighting for his life this time.

"Sure." Rory looked toward Marlie's closed door. "We should say hi."

Bosco snorted. During their days apart, he'd spent too much time thinking about his pretty neighbor. Way too much time. "You just want to see if she made dinner again." Although, he wouldn't mind seeing her. Just saying hi and being neighborly. Then he could forget all about the dream he'd had about her naked in his bed. Or the one with her nude over his couch. Also, the one on his kitchen table.

Rory happily stomped to her door and knocked.

"You're early." She opened it and then paused, still inserting a diamond earring into one lobe. "Oh, hi, Rory."

Her hazel gaze reached past him to Bosco. Was that relief in her pretty eyes? "Bosco. You're safe. I'm glad."

He nodded, turning for her apartment and trying not to drool at the formfitting red dress that crisscrossed on her chest to wrap around her throat. The waist was tiny with a wide band, and the soft material fell to right above her knees, showcasing shapely legs and four-inch fuck-me black heels.

His dick went hard as a rock, and he fought to keep his brain somewhat in charge. Where the hell was she going dressed like that on a Sunday night—like his best dream ever? "Hi. Rory wanted to beg for dinner."

She chuckled and turned away toward a small table.

The sound he made had his brother snorting away a laugh. The dress was backless. Completely. It fell in a V-shape to just above her curvy ass. He'd never seen anything so sexy. He swallowed.

She secured a silvery handbag and reached for her coat from the closet.

"Got a date?" Rory asked helpfully.

"Yeah." She patted her hair, which was up in a wild and curly mass that screamed *sex*. "It's a Christmas party at McDougal's Accounting Firm." She looked down at her dress. "I hope this is okay."

"You look gorgeous," Rory assured her. "Right, Bosco?"

Bosco nodded, shooting his brother a look that reminded him that he knew how to break a guy's neck with minimal effort. Of course, so did Rory. "Beautiful, Marlie. But it's cold outside." He reached for her heavy wool coat to bundle her in before he did something crazy like proposed. Or kidnapped her.

"The party will be inside," she said wryly, letting him fix the buttons. "But thanks."

A knock on the opened door had them all shifting.

"Turner," Marlie said, warmth in her voice.

"Hi." Turner was around six feet tall with lightish blond hair, deep blue eyes, and a square jaw that could probably take a punch.

He wore a black suit and handed over a bouquet of yellow roses. "I went for yellow. Red seemed too cliché."

Delight danced across her features. She blushed and accepted the flowers. "They're beautiful. Thank you. I'll go put them in a vase." She gestured toward Bosco. "This is my neighbor, Bosco Albertini, and his brother, Rory." She moved easily on those killer heels to the kitchen.

Turner's gaze dropped to the shoes, and he swallowed audibly.

Bosco hated him. Full on, full force, right there. The woman had only been in town a damn week, and she was already going on dates? "Bosco. The *neighbor*." He reached out and shook hands, almost keeping his squeeze casual.

Turner had a decent grip, as well. "Turner Johnson. It's nice to meet you." He also shook hands with Rory.

"What time do you think you'll have her back tonight?" Bosco asked.

Amusement lit Rory's eyes, but he kept his expression merely curious.

Marlie caught the comment as she returned. "Don't wait up, *Dad*."

The woman was two seconds from being tossed into a closet. Yeah, Bosco knew he had no right to even be thinking like that. "Darlin', you're new to town. I don't know Turner." He lowered his chin and met Turner's knowing gaze. "Now, I do." In the Albertini family, if somebody didn't have a family to watch out for them, they suddenly *did*. "Got me?"

Turner almost smiled. "Oh, I've got you."

Yeah, Bosco didn't like that connotation.

Rory threw an arm over his shoulder. "You kids have fun tonight." Then he pulled Bosco out the door toward his apartment, his grip tight. Once he had him inside, he shut the door and let go. "Dude."

"What?"

Rory pushed him even farther into the lonely and silent apartment, away from the keyhole. "Make up your mind."

"Already have." Bosco prowled across the living room to the tall handmade bar gifted to him by his Uncle Sean in order to pour two healthy shots of whiskey.

Rory sighed. "Rough mission? You're home earlier than I thought."

"The air refueling went well," Bosco handed one glass to his brother. "But things are gearing up, as you know, and I'll be heading out again soon."

"It's your job, and you love it." Rory tipped back the drink. "Doesn't mean you can't have a personal life."

"I used to think that, too," Bosco admitted. He loved air refueling planes while traveling around the world. "Jennie taught me otherwise."

Rory nodded. "Jennie is a nice woman who's looking for something else and that's okay. What's your plan with your sexy neighbor? I wasn't loving the vibe from Turner, and we do have several cousins we could set her up with if you're not interested. She's alone in town, and I don't like it."

Bosco tilted his head, not liking the heat filtering through his blood. "Why don't you ask her out?"

Rory studied him. "Well, now," he drawled. "That was quite the reaction. You get off your ass and ask her out. Besides, you know I have my hands full. Serenity is going to come to her senses soon."

"Timing isn't good," Bosco admitted. The timing wouldn't be good for years.

"That woman isn't going to wait for you if she is interested. She might've taken one look at your ugly mug and tossed you instantly into the friend zone. Sorry I got all the good looks."

Bosco rolled his eyes, his gut churning. Marlie had looked both delicate and beautiful in that red dress. He didn't like the dual sense of possessiveness and protectiveness that slammed through him.

He didn't deserve to feel either for his lovely neighbor.

HER FEET THROBBED, her temples ached, and even her shoulders hurt with a tightness that might require a deep-tissue massage later that week. Marlie gingerly wiped snow off the bottom of her heels before walking down the hallway toward her door. So close. Her comfy socks, pajamas, and maybe a chocolate bar were so close. Just mere feet away. "Turner, thanks for walking me inside, but I can make it from here."

"Of course, not." He still had his hand wrapped around her arm, and she felt the heat through her coat. "I have to make sure you're safely inside." Even after a cocktail party, a full dinner, dancing, and then after-dinner drinks at a small and way-too-smoky bar on the other side of town with a couple of other accountants who hadn't attended the party, Turner seemed full of energy and ready to go. Wasn't smoking in bars illegal? She hadn't even been able to see the place very well. Had just shut her eyes and almost fell asleep in the booth after they'd started talking about numbers, of all things.

She wanted to go...to bed. Like right now—and by herself.

"I had a good time tonight," he said, reaching for the key already in her hand.

"Me, too." She tried to smile but wasn't feeling it. The party had been fun, but he'd spent too much time ripping the other accountants apart after being nice to their faces. Then he'd held her too tightly on the dance floor, and while she'd been ready for a kiss, definitely not the one he'd tried to take deeper while dancing in front of a bunch of people she'd just met.

His hand on her butt had been the final straw, and that had ended things there.

"I can make my own way in," she said, keeping a death grip on the key.

"Well." He moved closer, his eyes dark. "This is our third date, you know."

She stumbled and then caught her balance without grabbing his arm. "Third date?"

"Sure." He leaned against the wall by the nicely shut door. "When we met at the coffee shop, and I bought your coffee could be considered our first date. Then lunch two days ago. Finally, tonight was a great time."

Meh. It was an okay time, and one of his friends at the after-dinner bar had been a creep who wouldn't stop looking at her boobs. Plus, they'd talked business for nearly an hour, and none of it had made any sense to her. They were all too drunk to be talking business anyway, especially about clients and their money, things which should've been confidential. She might've drifted off a bit. "Well, thanks for the third date," she said cheerfully. "I really need to get to bed now." The words were out before she caught herself.

"About that." He leaned in again and pressed his lips against hers. She kissed him back, wondering.

Nope. No connection. When Marlie backed away, she forced a smile. "Thanks again for the roses, Turner." The guy was not getting the hint.

He grasped her arm and pulled her closer, forcing her to plant a hand on his chest for balance and to hold him back. His torso wasn't nearly as muscled as Bosco's. "I want to come inside, Marlie. Thought I'd make that very clear."

She sighed. "No." Apparently, she needed to make things very clear, too.

"Yes." He tucked a hand around her waist, tugging her closer.

Annoyance filtered through her, and she stepped closer, her heel on the top of his shoe. Then she planted with all her weight.

He hissed and yanked his foot free. "That wasn't nice."

"*I'm* not nice," she admitted freely. "Time to let go of me, Turner."

"No." He yanked harder, pressing against her and reaching for her keys.

She pulled her hand away, for the first time feeling a sense of panic. It was well after midnight, and she was alone with him in the hallway. "Listen—"

He kissed her again, his mouth hard.

This time, she struggled in earnest, kicking his shin and ripping her mouth free. "Stop—"

Then he was across the hall, hitting the wall with the sound of a bat cracking a baseball. Bosco Albertini stood over him, fury vibrating along his very bare and muscled back. His door was wide open.

Without making a sound, he grabbed Turner around the neck, yanked him to his feet, and slammed him down again. Turner landed flat on his back, his chest heaving.

Bosco went down on one knee, his hand still around Turner's neck as Turner started to turn an alarming shade of red. Bosco had ALBERTINI tattooed across the top of his back and some sort of military tattoo on his bulging right biceps. His hair was mussed and his torso was iron-hard.

Turner clutched at Bosco's wrist, kicking up but not moving much.

"Stop," Bosco said, command in every line of his body.

Turner subsided, red striations cutting through the whites of his blue eyes.

"Did she say no?" Bosco snarled.

Turner paused but didn't say anything.

Bosco must've tightened his hold on Turner's neck because the guy gasped, and panic had him struggling again. Then Bosco lightened up. "Not going to ask you again."

"She said no." Turner gasped, tears leaking from his left eye.

"Got it." Bosco released the guy's neck, grabbed his thick hair, and pulled him to stand. Then he turned and shoved Turner toward the door, following him while only wearing unbuttoned faded jeans, his feet bare. "I'll be right back."

"No, wait—" Marlie finally found her voice. It was snowing outside, and the ground was already covered.

He cut her a furious golden-brown glare. "Stay. Here." He opened the door and tossed Turner outside into the lightly falling snow. "I'll deal with you in a minute, Marlie." Then he followed Turner and slammed the door behind him.

She froze. Just completely froze. Bosco had turned so casually violent that she wasn't sure how to react. He'd been saving her, and that was sweet. But right now, he was probably beating the crap out of Turner.

Violence didn't solve anything.

A few minutes later, Bosco stormed back inside, his feet and chest slightly red from the cold, and his eyes blazing hot. He wasn't covered in blood, so that was good. However, the knuckles on his right hand looked as if they were swelling.

She backed against her door, her eyes wide and her heart thundering. It was the most alive she'd felt all night, and all of a sudden, she wasn't tired a bit.

He reached her, and even though snow clung to his thick hair and bare shoulders, heat poured off him. "Are you all right?"

Numbly, she nodded, looking up about a foot at his furious face.

"You going to give me crap about being able to handle that yourself and say that I shouldn't have interfered?" He stood so close that her heart rate would not slow down.

She blinked. "Thank you for helping me."

His head lifted. "You're thanking me?"

She nodded. "Yeah. I wasn't doing a very good job of getting through to him, and you took care of it easily. I appreciate it." Her voice was all breathy, and her body felt tingly.

He frowned. "I wasn't expecting that." Then he looked at her like he really saw her. "You're welcome, but we're not finished with this conversation."

Yeah, he was right. Full-on correct. She leaped for him, wrapping both arms around his neck, and planted her mouth right on his.

Chapter Six

F ire exploded through Bosco so quickly his ears rang. With the adrenaline from the fight coursing through his veins and the fury beating in his heart, the kiss nearly dropped him to his knees. Instead, he caught her with an arm around her waist to keep her from falling after impacting him.

Then he kissed her back.

Taking over, taking control, he pivoted and put her butt to her door, accepting all she offered. She tasted like bourbon and honey and something so sweet he'd never get enough. His body pulsed with hunger.

Bourbon. Honey. Well after midnight.

He twisted his head away, keeping her safely in front of her door, his chest heaving. "Wait."

"No wait." She tried to climb inside his skin, leaning up on those dangerous heels to kiss beneath his jaw.

The woman was going to kill him. Forget terrorists. Forget the danger of flying planes so close they could refuel in the air. Forget even helping out with search and rescue fighting Mother Nature. Sweet Marlie Kreuk would do him in.

"No." He grasped her arms, careful to keep his hold gentle. "Wait a minute."

She blinked up at him, her sparkling eyes more green than brown. Needy and hungry eyes. For him. "Why?"

There were a million reasons why, but only one mattered right now. "How much have you had to drink?"

She blinked, and then the sweetest smile tipped her lips. "You are such a protective hero."

Hero? No. Protective? Yeah, probably. "Answer the question, sweets."

"I had one wine with dinner and then an after-dinner drink hours later that has not gone to my head. I'm fine. Sober. Fully in control of my faculties." Her gaze dropped to his mouth. "You can kiss, Albertini."

This was a colossal mistake.

She unbuttoned her coat, so close he felt the backs of her knuckles against the bare skin on his abs. It fell to the floor, along with her sparkly silver purse.

That breath-stealing dress and those heels were right there. So close. As if she knew the struggle he faced, she took the final step separating them, brushing her nails across his abs. "If you really don't want this, tell me, and I'll go inside my apartment and lock the door, perfectly safe. I'm not going to push you anymore."

Her mere existence pushed him to do something he shouldn't. Add in that dress, and he was lost.

He indulged himself by reaching for the clip in her hair, twisting it, and letting those curls cascade down over her shoulders. "This won't change anything, Marlie. My job still takes precedence, and I'm not a good bet."

"I'm not a gambler." She ran her fingertips up over his pecs to his neck and then into the thickness of the hair at his nape. "I'm not asking for anything from you. Except maybe one more kiss." She looked up and then stumbled a little in the high heels. Peach color wound through her face. "It's been a long night on these."

He caught her, his hand flattening across her lower back—her bare, soft, narrow lower back.

With that one touch, he was lost.

He slid his arm all the way around her waist, clamped a hand on her hip, and lifted her against him. She met his mouth more than halfway, and he took her deep, finally kissing her as he wanted. Full on, in control, learning everything he could about her.

She kissed him back, wrapping her arms around his neck and lifting her thighs to balance better against him. He turned, still kissing her, and stalked back into his apartment, kicking the door shut behind them.

Knowing the layout of his place in the dark, he maneuvered them to his bedroom, where he set her on her feet and then spun her around to face the wall.

Her laugh caught him in the balls, hard. Even so, he took his time, wandering his fingers down her exposed spine. "This dress should be illegal," he ground out, noting the fine globes of her ass in the flimsy material.

She turned then to face him, and he let her. "So should your abs." She tucked her fingers in them, spreading her hands out.

He reached behind her neck and unfastened the snap, unfolding the material and pushing it down to her waist. While she hadn't worn a bra, she had twin sticky pads over her hardened nipples that he gently lifted away.

Her soft gasp had him lowering his head to lick and kiss one before easing the pain in the other one. She shifted against him, her nails digging into his shoulders. "Bosco."

He lowered the dress to the floor, lifting first one leg and then the other to release them. Her panties were a sheer black that nearly killed him, and he removed them just as fast, wanting his mouth on her. Now.

Then he gently tossed her back onto the bed with one push.

She landed, her legs kicking out, her chuckle sweet. "My shoes."

"Oh, you're leaving those on, darlin'." He knelt, shoved his shoulders between her thighs, and then settled in for some fun.

She squirmed and tried to fight him, but he licked her and then sucked her clit into his mouth, his tongue still working her. Her nails clutched his bedspread, and she moaned, opening more for him. Her gasps spurred him on.

She tasted like sweetness with a hint of spice, and all of a sudden, he never wanted to be anywhere else. He slipped a finger inside her and moved faster, feeling her body stiffen and fight him. Battling the orgasm.

He chuckled and sucked harder.

Turned out she was a screamer.

MARLIE COULDN'T BREATHE. That had been the best orgasm of her entire life, and yet, she still needed more.

Bosco moved up her, kissing her hipbones, her belly, and then took his time with both breasts. His mouth was hot, and his tongue wickedly accurate. Finally, she reached down for his jeans. "Get these off."

He kept kissing her, nipping at her breasts, and then shoved the offending denim off.

Skin against skin nearly had her growling. Her fingers clutched in his thick hair, and she pulled. "Up here."

He scraped his teeth along her jaw before kissing her again. "You're kinda bossy in bed," he murmured, levering over her, so big and strong.

She swallowed, looking up into those bronzed Italian eyes. His cock pulsed against her sex, and she moved against him, letting sparks fly between them. "Am not."

"Are, too." He kissed her again, holding himself off her with his elbows. "I'm in charge here, sweetheart."

She didn't much care who was in charge so long as he stopped playing around. The guy seemed fine teasing her body, and he was driving her crazy. His sense of control was impressive. "Tell me you have condoms."

His grin was a bit lopsided, and the hunger that flared in his eyes a little intriguing—a lot intriguing, actually. "Yeah." His mouth dropped to play with her ear as his hand moved to the bedside table, drawing out a condom. Quick movements had it rolled on, and he hadn't paused in exploring her face for one second. He reached her mouth again, kissing her, tasting like mint.

Bosco Albertini knew how to kiss.

Fire poured down her throat to land in her abdomen, flaring out to her sex. She shifted against him, lifting her knees.

His grin was wicked. "You ready?"

"Yes," she breathed, sliding her hands down his flanks.

Truly wicked. "I'm not." With a smooth motion, he grasped her rib cage and flipped her over.

She landed on her stomach and bounced, her head coming up. She grabbed the pillow. "What in the world?"

His hands roamed down her back, gently ticking across her butt. "I'm not done playing."

Heat and need combusted inside her, and she felt empty. Needy. Hungry. "Are you this freaking detailed with your job?" she moaned, letting her face rest on his pillow, turned to the side.

"I'd better be," he murmured, his breath hot against her neck.

She shivered.

"I've wanted to do this since I saw you in that dress." He kissed the top of her spine and then licked his way down to her waist, leaving a hot trail of kisses, as well. Then both hands went to her butt, cupping her.

God, it was too much.

She swallowed. "Bosco. Foreplay later?" Her voice was way too breathy, and her body was on fire. For him.

"Definitely more later. A lot more." He nipped her butt.

That was it. She pushed up and rolled over, sliding under him and grabbing muscled arms. She wrapped both legs around his waist and pulled, digging in her nails.

His chuckle was pure sin.

"So impatient. You're beautiful, Marlie." He lowered his forehead to hers and slowly penetrated her, inch by inch, letting her body accept him. When he was finally all the way inside her, he paused, letting the moment stretch.

"Bosco," she murmured, clenching around him.

Then he stopped playing. Finally.

Grabbing her hip, lifting her against him, he started to pound. Hard and fast and with impressive stamina, he forced her up quickly. She tumbled, crying his name as an orgasm washed through her with the power of a runaway train.

He didn't so much as pause.

She started climbing again, holding her breath. Heat washed through her limbs, tingling every nerve, seizing her lungs. She tried to meet his thrusts but instead ended up just holding on, knowing he'd get her there. His grip on her hip tightened, adding just one more sensation to the millions already bombarding her.

She looked into his fierce eyes, which were lit topaz in the night, full of masculine intensity. Her heart stuttered.

Then he changed his angle, just a bit, and she blew right off the edge and into the storm. Crying out, she shut her eyes, letting the orgasm take her.

He hammered harder inside her, increasing the waves, until finally jerking hard with his own release.

She panted and came down, her breath catching and her mind spinning and numb. "Wow," she whispered.

His chuckle against her temple warmed her entire face.

Her heart turned right over.

Uh oh.

Chapter Seven

What had he done? Besides having the best night of his adult life and the best sleep... He'd wrapped himself around Marlie all night, awakening her twice for more mind-blowing sex before going back to sleep. Now, he was giving her some privacy in the bathroom as he gathered his senses. He paced in his kitchen, opening the fridge to see leftovers from his nonna. At hearing a noise, he turned to see Marlie in one of his faded T-shirts and a pair of boxers, her feet bare and her red dress in her hands.

"I didn't want to put this back on." Her blush matched her dress.

He straightened. "All I have is leftover spaghetti with meat-balls." He should at least feed her.

She smiled, looking young and fragile without makeup and her hair all over from his hands the night before. "That's okay. I'm good."

He moved then, straight at her, gathering her against his bare chest. She felt so freaking right in his arms. "You okay?"

"Yeah." Her voice was muffled, and she looked up, her head barely grazing his chin. "Are you?"

"Better than okay." The overwhelming sense of possessiveness striking through him would abate soon, right? He wanted her again and right now. Maybe he could think of a way—

A knock on the door brought him up short.

He released her and moved for it. Nobody was scheduled to pop by, and he didn't have to be on the base until noon. Hopefully, one of his brothers had just brought coffee. Opening the door, his gut sank. "Jennie."

She stood there in her pink coat and snowy boots with two lattes in her hands. "Hi. I hope it's okay that I dropped by."

Oh, shit.

Marlie was suddenly beside him, her face more of a crimson color now. "Um, hi. I was just leaving."

Jennie paled and stepped back.

Bosco swallowed, his ears ringing. "You don't have to leave." He wanted to stop her, but this was crazy.

"It's okay. I actually have a conference call with my division head in ten minutes." Marlie brushed by him, her feet and legs bare, wearing his clothing...and not looking at his face.

He blanched at seeing her purse and coat on the floor by her doorway. Had they just left those there the night before?

She grabbed her belongings, dug out a key, and unlocked her door.

He couldn't let this happen. "Marlie, I—"

She escaped inside her apartment and shut the door, not looking his way once.

Jennie watched her and then winced. "Our timing always sucked."

"Yeah," he said, staring at the closed door. Then he stepped back. "Come on in." Why did he feel like he was cheating on Marlie by letting Jennie into his apartment? He and Jennie had decided to be friends, right?

"Thanks." Jennie walked inside and kicked off her boots,

heading right for his sofa to set down the lattes. "So, this is totally awkward."

He finally let himself relax and prowled for the adjacent chair, reaching for a latte and swallowing down half of it before his butt even hit the cushion.

Jennie settled on the sofa, her blond hair up in a ponytail and covered lightly by snow. She slid out of her coat, revealing a pink sweater over dark jeans. "I—" She cleared her throat. "Who was that woman, Bosco?"

He took another drink. Not in a million years would he discuss Marlie with her. "I appreciate the coffee but need to get ready for work. What's up?"

She shifted uneasily on the sofa. "I've been thinking ever since we met up at the Clumsy Penguin the other night, and—"

"Jennie. Come on," he said as gently as he could.

She set her latte down. "I was wrong to end things. We were good together. You know we were."

Yeah, they had been. But even then, something was missing. His gaze moved toward his door and then back to her. "We tried three times." They'd get into a rhythm, his job would call, and he'd have to leave. She'd put on a brave face each time and then break up with him while he was away, saying that she couldn't handle it. He understood. Still did. Wasn't going there again. "We're just friends, Jennie. It's all we can be." However, she was a good reminder right then about his choices and his job.

She flushed. "You didn't have to move on so quickly."

He wasn't going there with her. "We broke up six months ago —for the final time. It was the right decision for us both." He looked over his shoulder at the clock on the microwave. "I want the best for you." It was the truth. He stood.

His door opened, and Rory walked inside, looking from Jennie on the sofa to Bosco's bare chest and unbuttoned jeans. "Come on."

Jennie stood and yanked on her jacket before stomping into her boots. "As always, it's good to see you, Rory," she snapped.

Rory shook his head. Then he stalked to the kitchen and opened the fridge door, ignoring them both. He rustled around and dug out an orange that looked a little green.

Bosco ushered Jennie to the still open door. "Thanks again for the coffee," he said.

She turned and slid her hands up his chest.

He took an immediate step back.

Her arms dropped. "Just think about it," she murmured, glancing toward Marlie's door and then back.

"No," he said. "Take care of yourself, Jennie." Then he shut the door and turned to look at his brother.

Rory tossed the orange into the garbage. "Have you lost your mind?" His eyes swirled an irritated hue.

"Maybe," Bosco allowed. "But not like you think." This was the perfect reminder of why he didn't have space in his life for a relationship, regardless of Marlie's appeal.

Even so, all he wanted to do was march to her apartment and make sure she was all right. "I have to get out of here. Want to go to breakfast?"

"You're buying, numbnuts," Rory retorted, heading for the door. "Should we invite Marlie?"

"No," Bosco growled. He needed time to think, away from his sexy neighbor.

MARLIE TIPTOED beyond Bosco's door, breathing a sigh as she reached the snowstorm outside. After returning to her apartment, she'd taken a quick shower and prepared to get organized for the day when her phone buzzed with a call from Anna Albertini to meet for brunch.

She reached her car and pulled away from the curb, calling

Anna. "I'm on my way. But I was thinking, weren't dead bodies showing up around you or something like that?" Yeah, her mind had been so full of Bosco, their crazy night of sex, and then Jennie on the doorstep that she'd forgotten all about Anna's problems and her being carried out by Aiden just the day before.

Anna chuckled over the line. "Yeah, but it was actually a misunderstanding, and they have the guy in custody. Honest. I'm not in any more danger than usual."

Than usual? At this point, Marlie didn't care. She knew one woman in this town who could potentially be considered a friend, and Anna was it. "I'm almost there." They were meeting at Smiley's Diner, which was just a few blocks from Marlie's apartment.

"Me, too." Anna clicked off.

Marlie found a parking spot by the curb and slushed through the billowing snow into the diner, instantly relaxing as the smell of homemade apple pie hit her. Her stomach growled, and she moved down the counter to a nice clean booth in the back, sliding in and shucking her coat.

The bell over the door rang, and Anna walked in, shaking snow out of her thick hair. She spotted Marlie and made a beeline to sit across from her. Today she wore a navy-blue suit with a pretty pink blouse. Stunning sapphires sparkled from her ears. She pulled out of her wool coat and set it on the seat next to her. "Morning."

"Hi." Marlie straightened her green sweater. "I like your suit. What do you do, anyway?"

"I'm a lawyer," Anna said, brushing more snow off her skirt. "What about you?"

"I teach at the college. Or I will when the spring semester starts in a few weeks." Marlie paused as a pretty woman with reddish-blond hair and deep green eyes brought over a coffee pot and turned over their cups.

The woman started to pour. "Mom called and said Nick's

grandma was making noises about us dating. You need to talk to him."

Anna nodded. "And say what?"

The waitress stiffened. "To knock it off. I don't want anything to do with him."

Anna's grin revealed that dimple. "Marlie, please meet my sister, Tessa. Who has a crush on Nick Basanelli and should stop hiding it."

Tessa smiled, and the resemblance between the two women became noticeable. "Hi. It's nice to meet you. You live next to Bosco, right?"

Man, it was a small town, and the Albertini family seemed to have zero secrets. "Yeah. It's nice to meet you, too." Marlie reached gratefully for the cup of coffee and took a sip. Delicious. "Who's Nick?"

"Nobody," Tessa said firmly.

Ah. It was like that, was it? "I get it," Marlie said honestly.

Anna rolled her eyes. "Nick is the prosecuting attorney, and we once worked together. Tessa blushes when we talk about Nick, he gets cranky when I talk about Tessa, and if you ask me, they should just get a room and work out their frustrations."

"You sound like Nonna," Tessa groused, turning her attention on Marlie. "You just missed Bosco and Rory. They had breakfast."

Heat filtered into Marlie's face. Her thighs were still whisker-burned from the man.

Tessa patted her shoulder. "Yeah. I thought so. Bosco is a great guy, but if you can't handle his job, then let him go."

"I don't have him," Marlie burst out and then calmed herself. "I can handle any job, but we're not dating." The monkey-sex night notwithstanding. "When a guy tells you you're just friends, you believe him. It's that simple." Yeah, she'd forgotten that last night, but it was a one-time thing—no matter how great the jackass was in bed. "Right?"

Both Albertini women nodded. "Yeah," Anna said. "Definitely."

Tessa's gaze narrowed. "Of course, men are morons."

Marlie ticked her head. "You're not wrong."

The door burst open, and the man in question stomped toward them, scattering snow. "I saw your cars. What the hell are you two doing having brunch like there isn't an insane stalker leaving Anna bodies?"

Marlie's breath seized. Wow. Bosco Albertini in a full temper was a sight to see. He looked broad and dangerous in his muted green jacket and faded jeans. His eyes blazed a wild amber, and he had his jaw clenched tightly enough to show off his tough-guy neck. "Um," she whispered.

"Um, nothing." He reached around Tessa for Marlie's arm. "Out of here. Now."

Anna snorted.

He turned on her while starting to pull Marlie from the booth. "Get your ass up and move. Now."

Anna's snort turned to chuckles, although her grayish-green eyes narrowed dangerously. "Listen, cousin. I have one man already bossing me around, and since he provides phenomenal orgasms, I let him. You, on the other hand, are about to get your butt kicked."

Bosco blanched. "Geez. Don't talk about sex with me. I like Aiden Devlin and don't want to have to kill him."

The little bell jangled, and Tessa looked toward the door. She winced, took a step away from the table, and sighed. "Oh, crap. You've done it now."

In unison, all three of them turned to see an older woman walk inside while pulling a snowy scarf off her head. She looked like a modern-day Sophia Loren as she turned and stared at them. Then she made a beeline their way, her rubber boots squeaking on the tiles. "Hello."

A perfectly choreographed sigh emerged from the Albertinis.

Bosco kept pulling Marlie. "Nonna? We need to get out of here. Right now."

Anna shook her head. "My case if fine and you need to mind your own business. Everyone is safe, Bosco." She tilted her head. "Including the woman you're currently manhandling."

Nonna pulled a wooden spoon from her purse. "Bosco? Are you manhandling your neighbor?"

Bosco immediately released Marlie.

Why was it *not* a surprise that this Nonna already knew who exactly Marlie was? Marlie bit back a smile. "You must be the famous Nonna of the Christmas decorations and wine. I'm Marlie. It's nice to meet you."

Nonna's smile lit up the entire restaurant. "It's so nice to meet you, too. I've heard that you speak Italian. Let's talk." She shoved Anna over with a hip and sat in the booth.

Bosco's groan wasn't nearly as silent as he no doubt wished for it to be.

Chapter Eight

M arlie tossed and turned in her bed, her mind refusing to relax. After an entertaining brunch with Bosco's Nonna and cousins, she'd driven through the storm to the college and organized her office before heading home and eating leftovers. Bosco had taken off for work the second Nonna told him to get lost at the diner, and he apparently hadn't come home yet.

Or if he had, he hadn't knocked on her door for a nightcap.

Which was good because they were just friends, and one night of sex didn't change that. Great sex. But even so, enough was enough.

She punched her pillow and rolled over, trying to get comfortable. The lightly falling snow outside had turned to a billowing blizzard, and ice scattered against her windows, making her snuggle down even more in her warm bed. The wind keened and tried to get inside, but the ice-crusted windows kept the chill outside.

A shuffling sound came from her living room.

She paused and turned over. Had something fallen? Her heart rate kicked up, and her body froze. Then she listened. Nothing. No sound. Geez. She was losing it. Even so, she remained alert, just like any woman living alone would. Then she slowly started to relax.

Her eyelids drifted shut.

Another sound.

She jerked fully awake, silently sitting up in bed while clutching the covers with her fingers. That was a real sound. She tilted her head, staying quiet. Was it just the storm against the windows? Yeah, she was probably paranoid.

Even so, she lifted the covers and set her feet on the chilly wood floor, gaining her balance before moving forward silently. She held her breath and reached the open doorway, sliding to the side to peer down the hallway to the living room. Shadows danced from the windows, and darkness edged from every corner, but the sparkling lights from the Christmas tree provided enough illumination that she could see the area.

Silently, she turned her head to hear better.

No sound. No breathing. No noise.

The atmosphere thickened around her. She had a very healthy imagination, and noises had awakened her before, only to turn out to be nothing. Even so, she held her breath and listened. Another shuffle.

Crap. That was *something*. A real noise.

Her heart thundering, she backed away from the door, watching the living room. A dark figure crossed in front of the Christmas tree, face covered by a ski mask.

Panic ripped into her skin. Her knees wobbled. She grabbed for the cell phone behind her on the bedside table, and the figure turned, staring right at her. It was a man, and he looked big in shadow. Black leather gloves covered his hands. She pulled the phone in front of her and started to dial 9-1-1. The guy rushed her, leaping inside her room and taking her down to the bed. The phone flew across the room to hit the wall.

She screamed, high and loud, kicking and punching. She scratched for his mask and tried to rip it over his head. He grabbed her neck with both hands and started to cut off her airway.

Her knee shot up, nailing him in the groin.

He groaned and loosened his hold.

She screamed again, frantically fighting him.

He grabbed something from his pocket, and then silver glinted. The blade was instantly against her neck, and she stilled, gasping for breath and trying to see his eyes. "Stop," he hissed.

She stopped fighting and sought an opening. With the blade against her neck, she couldn't move without getting cut. Even so, if he wanted her dead, he would've already sliced her throat. Panic heated through her, and her head buzzed. She blinked several times, grounding herself in the moment—so she could fight.

He yanked what looked like heavy tape from his back pocket.

The outside door crashed open, and they both jumped. The knife pricked her skin, and warm blood ran down her neck. She gasped and tried not to move as the pain slid through her. How deep was the cut?

He partially turned his head. "Shit. Plan B, then." He lifted the knife and plunged the blade toward her chest.

She twisted at the last minute and lifted her arm. Pain slashed through her, and blood arced. She screamed again, and darkness swam across her vision.

Then he jumped off her and pivoted, the knife glinting in the dim light. Two bodies impacted with a deep thud. A grunt of pain echoed through the room. Something hard hit the floor, sounding like it smashed the wooden planks in two.

Everything swam around her and then went dark, barely coming back into focus, her stomach lurching. What was happening? She needed to run. Her arm and neck hurt, and she felt dizzy. Even so, she tried to shove herself to a seated position, ready to kick out again if needed.

Bosco was instantly by her side, leaning down, holding his stomach with one hand, his other to his ear with a phone. He barked a bunch of words that sounded garbled. He slid the phone somewhere out of her vision, bent over, and grabbed her pillow to press against her arm.

Pain bloomed through her, and she cried out.

"Hold on, baby. You'll be okay." He leaned to the side and twisted on her antique milk glass lamp. Soft light illuminated his fierce eyes and bare torso.

She caught sight of blood across his abdomen. The entire room wavered and darkened.

Then she passed out cold.

❄

BOSCO SAT on the examination table as the doctor finished stitching up his abs. Fury continued to run through him, but he remained still, listening intently in case Marlie needed him again. She was in the adjoining room, also being stitched up.

Detective Grant Pierce loped into the room, his casual jeans and sweater showing he'd been called out of bed. His blond hair was messy, and his green eyes were sharp. They'd run into each other several times last year or so because of Anna, and he seemed like a good cop. "How bad?"

"Just ten stitches," Bosco muttered. "How is Marlie?"

"Minor cuts on biceps and neck. Right now, she's getting stitches in her upper arm," Pierce said, pulling a worn notebook out of his back pocket. "I'm talking to you first. Tell me what happened from your perspective."

Bosco ran him through the events of the night, from hearing Marlie scream to having the blade cut across his abs.

"Was the guy stabbing or slicing?" Pierce asked casually.

"He tried to stab me, I countered, and he ended up just cutting me," Bosco said, holding back a wince as the doctor set a bandage in place over his wound. "He was more than ready to kill, and he wore a ski mask and gloves. I didn't recognize anything about him." Bosco pushed off the table. "I saw him try to kill Marlie, but she twisted and took the knife in the arm instead of the chest." It was a sight he'd never forget. "Then he stabbed me, I threw him into the door, and I had to call you and cover her wound. Couldn't go after the guy."

Pierce's eyebrows rose. "Any chance you hurt him?"

"Yeah," Bosco said, his ears heating with his temper. "I heard a bone break. Best guess is shoulder or arm because he was able to run out of there." He shook his legs out to stabilize his balance.

"We'll call it into all local hospitals and emergency care facilities," Pierce said, taking notes. "Description?"

Bosco cleared his mind to think. "Shorter than me by a couple of inches, so probably six feet. He had a slight beer gut but was strong, and he smelled like deodorant. No visible scars or tattoos, and he was quick with the knife but not trained or I'd be bleeding more than I am right now. He dropped duct tape on the floor when he fled."

Pierce nodded. "I have a team at her apartment now. How long has Marlie lived next to you?"

"Almost two weeks," Bosco said. "She just moved here, and from what she's said, I don't think she was fleeing from anybody. She has a new job at the college that'll start the second semester. A professor named Mark was at the bar the other night. He seemed interested in her."

Pierce nodded. "All right. I'll follow up with her on that. For now, do you know of any reason somebody would want to hurt your neighbor?"

"There was another guy who got handsy with her after a date. His name was Turner, but this wasn't Turner. He has a narrow chest and no beer belly." Bosco shook his head. "Other than that, she has been seen with Anna more than once."

Pierce stopped writing and lifted his head, his jaw setting. "Seriously?"

Bosco nodded, crossing around him into the hallway. "Yep."

Pierce stepped next to him, walking to the next examination room. "Who knows who's after Anna now? Somehow, that woman is a magnet for trouble."

Wasn't that the damn truth? "You need to interview her about her current cases," Bosco said, striding into Marlie's room.

"No kidding," Pierce muttered, right behind him.

Bosco stopped short. Marlie sat on the table, a bandage on her neck and a larger one on her upper arm. She looked small and delicate on the table with her legs hanging off and not coming close to touching the tiled floor. Her hazel eyes were wide with fear and pain, and shock sat on her fragile face.

Anger slammed into him again, and he shook it off, striding inside and pausing right next to her. "You okay?"

She swallowed. "The doctor just left to get my discharge papers." She sounded dazed.

He gently slid her silky hair out of her eyes. "You did a good job defending yourself."

She looked up at him, her gaze finally focusing. "I, well, thank you for coming in. You saved my life." Her eyes filled with tears.

"You saved yourself." He wanted to gather her into a hug but didn't want to break her, so he left her in place. For now. "This is Detective Pierce. He has a few questions for you."

"Right." She took a deep breath and looked over at the detective. "I was asleep, heard a noise, tried to call 9-1-1, and then he was on me. He had a knife and some duct tape." She paled and trailed off, her gaze going to the window and the storm outside.

Bosco cut Pierce a look.

Pierce nodded. "So he initially wanted to bind you?"

She paled even more. "Yes. I think so?" She looked at Bosco again. "But the front door crashed open before he could use it, and the guy said something about a Plan B. Then he tried to stab me." Her eyebrows drew down into a frown.

"Did you recognize him?" Pierce asked.

"No," she whispered. "He wore a mask. I think his eyes were

blue, but I'm not completely sure. It was so dark. And when he spoke, there was no accent. I didn't recognize his voice, either." She shivered, looking small in her little tank top and shorts.

A nurse with thick gray hair and squeaky tennis shoes bustled in with discharge papers to hand over.

"We need a blanket," Bosco said.

The woman reached into a drawer, bringing out a wrapped blue blanket. "She was hot earlier, probably from shock. It's abating now." The nurse took off the plastic and placed it gently on Marlie's legs. "You can stay the night here at the hospital if you'd rather," she said kindly.

Marlie shook her head. "Thanks, but I want to go home." She shivered again.

Pierce scribbled in his notebook. "Is there anybody you can think of who'd want to kidnap you?"

She shook her head, pulling the blanket up farther to her waist, even though she was sitting.

"How about Mark from the college?" Pierce asked.

Marlie frowned. "Of course, not. Bosco, how could you even think that? Mark is a nice guy."

Maybe or maybe not. "He still needs to be checked out." Bosco looked at Pierce. "There's also Turner."

She swallowed. "Turner is way thinner than the guy who attacked me. It wasn't him."

Good point. Bosco nodded. "I agree. Turner weighs far less." He looked at the detective. "You think this is about her, or is it random?"

Pierce made a few more notes. "I don't know. There are a couple of unsolved breaking and entering cases with rape in Spokane, but the victimology is different in that those women are older. However, I'll dig deeper with my colleagues across the border and see what we can come up with. I'll also talk to Anna about current cases, although I don't see how Marlie would be involved since she's new to town." He looked at

Marlie. "Do you have anybody you can stay with for the time being?"

She swallowed. "I'm fine."

"She has me," Bosco said, glancing at the clock on the wall. "If you need to talk to her some more, she'll be at my place."

Pierce studied them both. "I thought you said she moved in recently."

"I did," Bosco said softly.

Pierce sighed. "You Albertini men. I'm going to have to ask you a few more questions, Bosco."

Yeah, he'd figured.

Chapter Nine

Marlie let the heater in Bosco's passenger seat warm her legs as he parked the truck at the curb. They had made the way home in silence, both lost in thought. Plus, she had happily taken the pain pill offered by the doctor, and most of her body had gone nicely numb.

"Stay here." Without waiting for an answer, he jumped out and jogged through the blistering snow to open her door and lift her into his arms.

"I can walk," she said, snuggling against his bare chest. "I think I've seen you without a shirt more than with one since I moved in next door." Not that she was complaining. His hard-ass chest was something to look at, not to mention touch. She rubbed her cheek against his warm skin. The snow landed on him and melted instantly. "How are you not cold?"

He strode inside the building and moved instantly for his apartment, opening the door and setting her on her feet. "I run hot. Hold on a sec." He shut and locked the door before passing through the apartment as they did on television to clear rooms. Then he returned. "Want to argue?"

She swallowed, holding the hospital blanket around her chilled body. "About?"

"About your staying here for the night?" He cocked his head.

What kind of women had he dated? She shifted her feet on the cold floor. "Am I supposed to argue about that?" The last place in the world she wanted to be was back in her apartment by herself right now. Her face heated.

The flash of a grin was unexpected. "Yeah. We're just friends, and you're all independent, and you can take care of yourself. That argument."

"Oh." She tilted her head to study him. Yep. Sexy, hard body with a stubborn angle to his chin. "Would I win that argument?" Curiosity ticked through her.

"Nope. Not a chance," he said agreeably.

She exhaled slowly. "I don't want to go back to my apartment by myself tonight. In fact, my door is still busted down. I'm scared, and you make me feel safe." In fact, he had saved her. Twice now. "Does that make me weak?" She couldn't imagine Bosco Albertini with a weak woman.

"Do you think it makes you weak?" Now he sounded curious.

She shook her head. "I think it shows I have a brain. Right now, there's a guy out there who stabbed us both. You're a trained soldier, and you kicked his ass. I want to stay right here until we catch this guy or at least figure out who he is. But if you don't want me to, then I get it. We're just neighbors and probably friends, and you don't owe me anything." It was the truth. If he didn't want her there, she'd go to a motel. "I do have options. Safe ones."

"Your safest option is to stay with me," he drawled.

"Probably," she admitted. "But I also don't want to cause problems. Your ex-girlfriend showed up here with two lattes, wearing tight jeans. No doubt she wants to try to date you again. So, if you're going that route, it would be a huge mistake for me to stay the night here."

The idea of him getting back with Jennie was like a punch in her stomach, and Marlie needed to get a grip on that. Obviously, there was a messy history there, and maybe Bosco was still in love with the pretty blonde.

He reached for Marlie's hand and drew her farther into the darkened apartment. "Jennie and I are not getting back together, and I would very much like for you to stay here tonight. We can fix your door in the morning."

She tripped along, fighting a grin. "It's so nice of you to ask."

"Right?" He led her into the bedroom. "It seemed like we were already agreeing, so I didn't see a reason to get all bossy."

She did like a logical man. Heat blasted through her at looking at the bed they'd shared not too long ago. Oh, the things that Bosco could do in that bed. Right now, her body ached, and her eyelids were heavy. Without arguing, she slid beneath the covers and scooted to the far side, careful of her injured arm. "We're both sleeping here, right?" While he'd no doubt offer to take the sofa, she wanted him here.

"Yeah." He turned off the light and shucked his jeans, sliding in next to her. "Don't be scared."

She was. Oh, she didn't want to be, but that guy and his knife were still out there. "I'm not," she lied. Tears filled her eyes, and she started to shake.

"Oh, sweetheart." He drew her closer, wrapping his muscled arms around her. "Listen. You did a great job defending yourself, and you're safe. I'm not going to let anything happen to you. I promise."

She let the tears fall against his warm skin, wanting to have the right to cry on him. To depend on him. Not just because they were neighbors. The more time she spent with Bosco Albertini, the more time she didn't want to be anywhere else. "Thank you, Bos."

He kissed the top of her head. "It feels right having you here."

She blinked. "As friends."

He paused. "I don't know."

A smile slid through her, but she wasn't an idiot. "You're just overwhelmed by the night and by saving me. I'm sure you'll want to remain buddies as soon as daylight kicks up."

He chuckled. "You know, you're kind of hard on a guy's ego. Most women would've taken that opening."

Yeah. She wasn't most women—and again, not an idiot. A guy who looked like Bosco, acted like Bosco, was a soldier-hero like Bosco...had women falling all over him. "Sorry, buddy. You put me in the friend zone. That's where we'll stay," she whispered, not meaning a word of it.

If Bosco Albertini wanted her heart, he would have to work for it.

Yep. Not an moron.

After issuing that very definite challenge, she fell asleep in his arms, feeling safer than she had in years.

BOSCO FINISHED FLIPPING the pancakes and paused at hearing a sound in the adjacent apartment. He angled his head to make sure Marlie was still in the bathroom before pulling his gun from above the fridge and moving silently out his door to Marlie's place. He nudged her door open and then stilled, tucking the weapon into the back of his waistband. "You have got to be kidding me."

Nonna and Anna had finished cleaning up the mess left by the police the night before. While that was nice, the whiteboard they'd put up near the fireplace shot his temper into the stratosphere.

Anna held up both hands. She wore a light green skirt, white sweater, and fuzzy socks. "Aiden and I fixed the door earlier this morning, so it's all good now." Her shoes had been kicked near the sofa. "Nonna was coming, and I said I'd help." Her eyes implored him not to lose his mind. "I didn't want her to come alone."

Nonna looked over her shoulder at him. "Lose the attitude,

young man." She turned back to the whiteboard. "We're not letting this case get away from us."

Anna hung her head.

Movement sounded behind Bosco, and Marlie stepped up, angling to see around him. She'd taken the bandage off her neck, leaving a small scratch, and a thicker bandage showed on her upper arm. She wore his boxers and T-shirt again, looking delectable, fragile, and a little caught off guard. Her hair was up in a ponytail, and without makeup, she was lovely. "Um."

Yeah. Exactly. Bosco stepped across the threshold and pulled her inside the room, just in case. He didn't like her exposed in the hallway. "You've met Anna and Nonna."

"Hello, dear," Nonna said, pivoting by the whiteboard, which held a list of suspects. "We're going to help you figure this out."

Marlie hovered next to his side and read the board, which they had labeled: *Marlie Attack Case.* "Jennie is at the top of your suspect list?"

Bosco read through the list. Jennie was first, followed by *unnamed ex of Marlie*, then *unknown bad guy from Spokane*, '*Mark*,' '*Turner*' and then another question mark. It wasn't a bad list. "Nonna. I think the police have this covered."

Nonna's hair was up in an intricate knot, and her red glasses were perched halfway down her straight nose. Her brown eyes sparkled. "Maybe, but with the Albertini men, it's usually an ex who didn't want to let go. We solved the case for your brother last week, and I know we'll solve this one."

Anna blanched. "We didn't exactly solve the case, Nonna. Chrissy held Heather at gunpoint, remember?"

Bosco shook his head as irritation made his skin itch. Quint's ex, Chrissy, had gone after his new girlfriend, Heather. Chrissy was in custody, and everything was okay now. The family was hoping for an engagement by Valentine's Day. "Jennie did not take out a hit on Marlie last night. Trust me." Jennie might be ticked they weren't together, but she wouldn't do anything like that.

"I don't know," Nonna mused, tapping her red lips. "Jennie obviously has judgment issues if she let you get away."

Marlie snorted and then caught herself, coughing. "Mrs. Albertini, while I appreciate the help, Bosco has made it more than clear that we're just friends. There is no reason for any woman to decide I'm an obstacle."

Nonna's chin lowered. "Is that true, Bos?"

He tried so hard to keep his temper in check. "We did have that discussion, but it's private, Nonna. Please respect that."

She rolled her eyes. "Oh. I had not realized that fact." She smiled, all charm again. "In that case, Marlie, would you like to attend a family holiday party this Thursday night? I would love to introduce you to Knox, one of Bosco's brothers. When the Albertini men fall, it's pretty much instant. Knox is charming and quite dashing, if you ask me. Definitely takes after my side of the family."

Not in a million years. Bosco's chest heated, and he forced a smile. "Thank you for cleaning up the apartment, but you're both off the case. Anna, go back to work. Nonna, how about I drive you home?" He didn't want to leave Marlie without cover, but enough was enough. "Marlie can come with us."

"I can drive myself, thank you." Nonna walked to the sofa to fetch her jacket, handing it to him.

He dutifully helped her into the heavy wool. "I know."

Anna's eyes sparkled, and pure amusement filled her face.

Oh, he didn't think so. "You left off a line for another potential suspect on your case board, Nonna. It's quite possible that Marlie got caught up in one of Anna's law cases, and that's why somebody tried to kidnap her. Have you thought of that?"

Anna lost her smile.

Nonna turned toward her. "Well, no. I had *not* thought of that." She tossed Anna's coat toward her. "Let's get breakfast and discuss your current cases. Maybe there is an angle we hadn't considered."

If looks could shrivel a guy's balls, the one Anna shot him would do it.

He grinned, finally feeling amusement for the first time since he'd had to break down Marlie's door and deal with a jackass holding a knife. "That's a wonderful idea, Nonna. If you come up with anything, please let both the police and me know. I'd really appreciate it."

Nonna patted his chest and then winked at Marlie. "Not a problem. Marlie, real quick, did you leave an angry ex in Seattle?"

"No," Marlie said, looking a little dazed. Nonna had that effect on people. "My last relationship ended two years ago, and he married one of my friends. They just had a little girl." She stepped to the side. "Thank you for cleaning up the mess. I really appreciate it."

"Um, excuse me?" Turner Johnson edged in and handed Marlie a bouquet of yellow roses. He still sported the black eye Bosco had given him, and he moved as if his ribs continued to ache. Good. "I read the paper this morning about your attack and wanted to make sure you were okay."

Bosco really wanted to take the guy to the ground again. Like right now. Instead, he kept his body angled toward Marlie in a possessive stance that nobody could possibly miss.

Nonna pursed her lips. "Who are you?"

Turner held out his hand. "Turner Johnson. Marlie and I are, um, friends."

Nonna shook his hand and tapped her foot. "Ah ha. Where were you last night, young man?"

Turner gulped, his eyes widening. "I was in Portland on business and took the early flight to Spokane this morning. I read the newspaper at the airport and drove right here after getting flowers."

Nonna frowned, looking disappointed. "That's probably easy to prove."

Turner looked at Marlie and then back at Nonna. "Yes, ma'am. I stayed at the Portland Hotel, and it was quite nice."

Nonna sighed. "They probably have tons of security cameras."

Turner looked even more bewildered. "Yeah, they do." He looked at Marlie. "It wasn't me. You know that, right?"

She nodded. "Yeah. He wasn't as tall as you, and it wasn't you when he spoke. Don't worry, Turner."

"I'm not." Even so, Turner edged away from Nonna, looking like he seriously regretted bringing the flowers. "Um, if you need anything, give me a call." Then he made a quick escape.

Marlie looked down at the bouquet.

Nonna shook her head. "It's not him. I also don't think he'll be back. Marlie, I'll see you at the Christmas party on Thursday night so you can meet Knox. Anna will text you the address. Anna, let's go to breakfast and discuss your cases." She leaned up and kissed Bosco's cheek before sweeping into the hallway.

Anna followed. "I'm going to kill you, Bos," she muttered, moving past him.

Quiet descended. Marlie, flowers still in hand, looked up at him. "Your family is interesting."

He burst out laughing.

Chapter Ten

Marlie settled into the booth at Smiley's Diner with Rory Albertini across from her, typing rapidly on his phone. "I'm fairly certain I don't need a babysitter," she said for the third time.

Rory didn't look up from the screen. "Bosco had to head into the base for a couple of hours, which left you unprotected. So, we're having a nice lunch together."

They'd already ordered.

She looked toward the counter, where Mark turned from the register at the end, a bag of takeout in his hands. His dark hair was wind-blown, and he looked good wearing a new plaid jacket. She waved.

He glanced at Rory, nodded at her, and then winked. He moved toward the door and quickly exited.

She watched him go. Detective Pierce had called earlier after interviewing Mark, who had an alibi from a woman he'd picked up at a bar for the time of the attack. Pierce had seemed satisfied with the explanation, and Marlie would've known had the assailant been Mark.

Rory kept on typing away.

She sighed. "It's like we don't talk any longer, Rory. Here we are at a nice restaurant, already ordered food, and you're on your phone."

He blinked and looked up, his blue eyes narrowed. "Smart aleck."

She shrugged. "If you're forcing your presence on me, you should at least be present." Yeah, she was feeling a mite unsettled and cranky.

He set the phone to the side and focused on her. "Alrighty, then. How about you tell me what's going on between you and my younger brother?"

"By just one year," she retorted, wishing he'd go back to his phone.

He lifted one eyebrow, looking so much like Bosco that she wanted to sigh.

"How many of you Albertini brothers have brown eyes, and how many blue?" she wondered.

He grinned. "Three brown, two blue, one greenish-blue, and we all have brown to black hair. Now. You and Bos. What is up?"

"Nothing," she said honestly. "We decided to be friends."

Rory waved a hand in the air. "Don't be obtuse. You're more than friends, and you both know it. But I wanted to talk to you about that—just you and me for a couple of minutes." Any amusement fled his hard-edged face.

Fascinating. She leaned her chin on her hand. "Are you going to warn me off your brother?" She'd never been warned off by a family member before.

"Maybe." Rory's eyes held a darker blue rim around the blue iris. "Jennie messed with his head. When he's on a mission, away from home, he has to concentrate so he doesn't end up dead. If you can't handle his life, then get out of it now. Please."

Wow. That was direct. She reached for her water glass and took a sip. "Okay. Here it is, bossy butthead." How was she going to put this? "Your brother tossed me into the friend zone, and if he wants me elsewhere, he's going to have to ask nicely. If he does, and *if* I decide that I want to be more than friends, then you have nothing to worry about. I respect his job and would never want to change him."

Rory sat back. "He could die."

She shrugged. "I lost both of my parents, and they were just driving in a car. We could all die." She fiddled with the wrapper from her straw. "Bosco loves his job, and it seems like a part of him, and anybody with him would need to be all-in. I get that." Changing the guy would be a mistake. He was pretty great as he was, and if danger came with that, then so be it. "But again...just pals."

Rory grinned. "Okay."

She waited. "That's it?"

"Yep." Rory sat back as Tessa placed a club sandwich in front of him and a Cobb salad in front of Marlie.

Tessa looked them over. "Are you giving her the third-degree? If so, stop it. Bosco can take care of himself."

"Nope." Rory unfolded his paper napkin to set on his lap. "We're all good. They're both playing the we're-just-friends dance, and they're both really dumb, but I'm appeased. Tell Nonna that Operation Bosco is a go."

Marlie coughed. "Operation Bosco?"

Rory lifted a shoulder. "When an Albertini man falls, it's fast and hard. Bosco has dropped but doesn't know it yet. He's not the brightest among us."

Tessa punched him in the arm. "You're all morons."

Marlie slowly nodded. "I can't say that I disagree."

Rory happily dug into his sandwich.

Tessa straightened and a smile tipped her upper lip. "Speaking of which, Serenity just walked in."

Rory dropped the sandwich and turned toward the door, tension instantly vibrating from him.

Marlie struggled to breathe in the suddenly thick atmosphere, sliding to the edge of the booth so she could see the doorway.

A woman with long black hair, unreal green eyes, and a thick black coat covered with snow stood there, her gaze caught by Rory's. She steeled her shoulders and walked toward them, leaving smudges of snow on the floor.

"Damn," Tessa murmured, stepping closer to Marlie and vacating the center of the table. "Hi, Serenity," she said as the woman approached.

"Hi." Serenity didn't look away from Rory. "Stop calling me."

Rory frowned. "I haven't called you."

"Bullshit," the woman said, red spiraling through her cheeks. "One more time, Rory, and I mean it. You call and hang up again, and I'm calling the police. It's harassment."

Rory stood, instantly towering over the woman. "If I were harassing you, darlin', you'd know it."

Tessa nudged Marlie's shoulder. "Ever see an Albertini go caveman?" she whispered.

Marlie watched, fascinated. "I think Bosco has gone there a couple of times," she whispered back.

Serenity rolled her eyes, looked at Tessa, and then glared back at Rory. "You're all nuts. All of you." Then she turned on her heel and marched to the other side of the diner, reaching a group of women all looking on with wide eyes.

"We're not done with this conversation," Rory called out. "I've given you until the new year, and then we're having that talk."

The finger she shot him wasn't a nice one.

Rory sat back down.

Tessa frowned. "Have you been calling her?"

"No." He reached for his phone again. "But I'm gonna find out who has been."

※

Bosco picked Marlie up at the diner and drove her to the police department, uncharacteristically quiet. When she couldn't take it any longer, she turned toward him in his truck. "I'm moving back to my place tonight."

"No, you're not." He parked in a large lot and then cut off the engine.

She shifted uneasily on the seat. "Bosco. Enough. You're not responsible for me."

He turned to look at her, his gaze unreadable in the snowy day. "You came to me, you cried in my arms, and you're in now, baby. I am responsible for you until we find this guy. Fight me all you want, but you're not gonna win." He opened his door and shut it sharply.

Her mouth gaped open, and she quickly smacked her lips together before opening her door. He, of course, was already there waiting to help her down onto the icy asphalt. "Listen. I do not go for the bossy type."

"You do in bed." He shut the door and ushered her to the sidewalk and around frozen rose bushes toward a larger brick building.

Oh, he had not just said that. She yanked her arm free and strode up the steps and into a warm entryway with a police officer sitting behind a counter. The guy was young, red-headed, and freckled. He looked up and smiled.

She returned the smile. "Hi. I'm Marlie Kreuk. I am supposed to meet with Detective Pierce." The detective had called earlier and asked for her to come by.

"Sure thing. Go to the second floor, turn left, and you'll find his office to the right," the deputy said.

"Thanks." Marlie turned and headed up the stairs, ignoring the solid form of masculine stubbornness dogging her every move. "I don't need your help."

"Too bad," Bosco said shortly.

She paused at the top and swiveled to face him. "I don't know why you're in such a bad mood, but if you want a fight, you're about to get one."

His eyes were a dark topaz beneath the fluorescent lights. "I don't want to fight." He grasped her arm and turned her toward an office where Detective Pierce was emerging.

The detective caught sight of them and motioned them forward. "Thanks for coming." He wore gray slacks, a pressed white shirt, and a blue power tie. With his blond hair and sizzling green eyes, he looked all business and fairly tough. "Come in."

She walked inside his office to take one of two guest chairs while Bosco sat next to her.

Pierce crossed around his desk, tossed a file folder on top of a bunch of other folders, and sat. "We dumped all the CCTV in the area and didn't find a vehicle or the guy who attacked you," he said without preamble. "I'm cross-referencing all of Anna's private cases right now and have found nothing to tie to the perp." He pulled a yellow legal pad from the bottom of the file folders and read quickly. "The MO is different than the guy attacking women in Spokane, but I'm not ruling him out."

Her heart sank. "So you have no idea who the man was who attacked us."

"No," Pierce said grimly. "In addition, I've confirmed Turner Johnson's alibi. The guy was in Portland that night, and he has no criminal record or any hint of problems."

"Great." Her voice shook, although she'd known Turner hadn't been the attacker.

Bosco reached for her hand and took it, warming every inch. "We'll find him."

"Your colleague Mark from the college still has a solid alibi. I double checked." Pierce looked at their joined hands and then lifted his gaze to Bosco. "Any chance this has something to do with you?"

"I don't see how," Bosco said quietly. "I guess anybody could've seen us together at the Clumsy Penguin, but nobody is after me. My work is far away from here, and I don't have any enemies."

"Any ex-girlfriends who could've hired the attacker?" Pierce asked.

Bosco shook his head. "No. Only ex is Jennie Newton, and she wouldn't do anything like that."

"Even so, I have to check up on her," Pierce said. "I'll call her in, so be prepared for some anger."

Bosco sighed. "Always. But I'm telling you, it wasn't her. So it's either the guy from Spokane or somebody else who randomly attacked Marlie."

Pierce studied Marlie. "Run me through everything he said again."

She did, holding tightly to Bosco's hand, their earlier argument forgotten.

Pierce sat back. "So he wanted to kidnap you, it sounds like. Then when Bosco broke in, the assailant decided to kill you." He shook his head. "The only way that makes sense is if that he wanted to ask you something. What could you know that somebody is afraid you know?" Pierce was sharp, that was for sure.

"Nothing," she whispered. "I teach languages at the college and haven't even started work yet. I don't know anything that would get somebody in trouble."

"Okay," Pierce said quietly. "Alternative theory. Somebody wanted to take you, maybe dispose of your body elsewhere, but when Bosco broke in, they had to attempt to kill you. If this is about Bosco, then his arrival would've changed things." Pierce watched Bosco carefully. "In theory one or theory two, somebody wants her dead. If the connection is to you, who would want her dead, Albertini?"

"Nobody," Bosco growled. "The only altercation I've had lately was with Turner Johnson, and you've cleared him. What if he hired one of his buddies to kidnap her?"

"Why?" Marlie asked. "That doesn't make sense. I had coffee, lunch, and then one true date with the guy, really. It wasn't that much fun, and once he sobered up the next day, he apologized for being a jerk."

Pierce nodded. "There isn't much time there for the guy to become obsessed to the point of having her kidnapped or killed." He rubbed his broad hand over his eyes. "This doesn't make sense. If somebody is obsessed with you, they wouldn't want you dead. Kidnapped, sure. But dead, no."

Marlie swallowed over the lump in her throat.

Pierce leaned forward. "All right. Run me through the entire night again. And again. We're going to figure this out."

Chapter Eleven

Bosco tossed the pizza box into the fridge and threw a treat to the dog. He'd picked up Fabio from Knox on the way home from the police station, figuring that having the dog close would make for a good alarm system. Plus, the canine seemed to calm Marlie, so that was a plus. "You didn't eat," he murmured.

She shrugged, looking bewildered and fragile sitting on his sofa with the scratch across her neck. "I'm not really hungry."

Neither was he, truth be told. "We're going to find this guy."

She looked up, her pretty eyes clouded. "Do you think the detective was right in that this is about you somehow?"

"I don't see how." He crossed around the sofa, stepped over the dog, and sat next to her. "I also don't see how it's about you. I think it's connected to the guy terrorizing Spokane, but I can't figure out how he saw you." He ran his fingers through her hair. "Unless he was at the Clumsy Penguin that first night and followed us from there." It was the only thing that made sense, but it didn't feel right. None of this did.

"Are you still mad at me?" She leaned into his touch, her foot buried beneath the huge mutt on the floor.

He eyed the dog. "I wasn't mad at you." His phone buzzed, and he lifted it to his ear. "Albertini."

"I cannot believe you called the police on me," Jennie yelled.

He winced and leaned forward, breaking his connection with Marlie. "I didn't. Honest. I know you didn't have anything to do with a crime, Jennie. I'm sorry."

Marlie shifted her weight. "Going to bed. Have fun." She headed into his bedroom and shut the door.

He looked at the closed door, his temper stirring. None of this was his fault, damn it. "Listen. I'm sorry."

Jennie sighed. "Honestly, Bos. How could you even give them my name? I spent an hour with Detective Pierce, and after that, I felt like I *had* done it. This is nuts."

"I know." He rubbed a hand across his jaw, every impulse alive inside him wanting to go into his bedroom. Now. "The police have to check all angles, and I wish you hadn't gotten caught up in all of this. I really do apologize."

"None of it makes sense," Jennie said, her voice a little slurred as if she'd been drinking—not that he could blame her. "Are you sure there was even an assailant? I mean, think about it. She has a crush on you, she gets attacked, and now you're her tough-guy guardian. You have a protective streak a mile long, Bosco."

He nudged the dog, who opened one eye to glare at him. "I threw the guy to the floor, Jennie. He was real. As are the stitches across my gut."

"Maybe Marlie hired him," she said quietly.

That was ridiculous. "The guy tried to kill her, Jennie. This isn't Marlie's fault any more than it's yours. Again, I'll try to keep you out of the rest of it."

"Is there any chance for us? Have you thought about it?" she asked, her voice soft.

"No." He'd never believed in lying to anybody. "There's no chance. You were right to break it off, and I hope we can stay friends." At that, they said their goodbyes.

He stood and angled toward his bedroom, knocking on the door before entering. Unlike Jennie, he wasn't letting this woman go. It was probably time to have that talk with her and see if he could repair the damage he'd done by giving her the friends speech right off the bat.

She sat on the bed, wearing leggings and a thick sweater, her gaze focused. "How's the ex? I can leave if you want her to come over." Sarcasm and more than a hint of temper lifted Marlie's consonants.

So, she wanted to play it like that, did she? He crossed his arms. "Knock it off. We need to talk."

She bounded to her feet, both hands going to her hips. Without the bandage, there was just a thin mark on her neck, although the bandage on her arm made her shirt bulge a bit. Though the injury didn't seem to be slowing her down much. "I am *so* done with you telling me what to do."

Okay. She was scared, she was angry, and she wanted to fight. Good enough. He looked down at her, trying not to smile. Man, she was adorable. "Listen. I was wrong to put you in the friend zone. I got burned by Jennie and thought I couldn't handle a relationship, but I want to try with you. I can look into other jobs in the military." He could give up the danger.

If anything, her eyes sparked even more while color infused her face. "Are you kidding me?" she yelled.

He almost took a step back. "No?" Why was she mad? He was making a serious effort here. "I'm not kidding." His temper stirred at the base of his neck.

"You are such a moron," she yelled, the decibels echoing off his walls.

Wait a minute. He'd just made a serious move, tried to compromise, and she was calling him names? "Baby, if you want to fight, you're headed in the right direction."

Instead of backing off, instead of pausing, she marched right up to him, anger in her gaze. "Let's go, then. You want to fight?

You've got it." She leaned up, still not coming close to eye level. "I don't want you to change. Anybody who asks you to change to be with them is an asshole. One thing I am not, is that."

He blinked.

"I like you the way you are," she yelled, her cheeks red and her mouth bow-shaped and much too enticing. "Except for the moron part. Get rid of that, and we have a chance."

That was it. He clamped a hand on her healthy arm, drew her into him, and kissed her.

Hard.

She moaned beneath his mouth as he consumed her, taking everything she offered and more. He backed her to the bed, careful of her injuries, drawing her sweater over her head as he went. Her hands slid to his belt, unbuckling it before unzipping his jeans.

Her tongue tangled with his, and the flavor of her—mint and woman—exploded on his tongue. His body went rock-hard as he removed her bra, shoving down her yoga pants in the same heartbeat.

Then he was on her for the briefest of seconds before rolling them until she was on top of him, frantically trying to shove his jeans down to his ankles. He helped her and then yanked his shirt off.

She paused, sitting up, square on his groin. The thin material of her panties and his boxers barely kept him from her. From being inside her, right where he needed to be. Her gaze softened, and her fingers ran along the top of his bandage. "I forgot. You're hurt."

"That's not where I hurt," he groaned, grasping her thigh and pressing her heated core down onto his aching cock.

She smiled, all sin. "Oh."

Yeah. Oh.

A wicked glint filled her eyes, and she leaned over, her mouth right above his. "I guess now we talk about you being an idiot?"

❄

SHE'D GONE TOO FAR. She knew it the second her mouth touched his, and those dangerous topaz-colored eyes flared hot and bright. One second, she was on top of him, in perfect control; and the next, she was under him. Completely.

Desire cut through her, and she gasped, looking up at him. He was so strong and intense, and everything inside her softened. She was already wet and ready for him.

His smirk held a hint of pain and a boatload of hunger. "You were saying?" He pressed against her, pulsing, his body hot and aroused.

Blood rushed through her head, making her ears ring. The man felt like heated stone against her that she didn't want to think —only feel. And, man, he made *her* feel good. "Um." What had she been saying?

He leaned to the side, his boxers disappeared, something crinkled, and he rolled partially away for a second. One strong hand snapped her panties in two, and he tossed them over his shoulder. Her eyes widened, and need coursed through her, painful with an edge. He positioned himself at her entrance and paused. "You sure?"

"Yes." She could not be more sure. Not in a million years.

"Me, too." Then he slowly, methodically, purposefully pushed inside her, his gaze on hers.

Wild and intense.

SHe couldn't breathe. Her thighs widened naturally, wanting more of him. Needing all of him.

He stretched her, changing her ache of need into a finely tuned edge of pleasure and pain. So good. His thighs were hard against hers, his skin warm, his scent masculine. Everything about him was perfect. Well, perfect for her.

"Bosco," she whispered, overcome. She'd never felt this good, this complete. Or this safe. Bosco Albertini was sexy and strong, but he made her feel safe and protected in a way she wanted. Maybe needed. Things were happening inside her too quickly, but she didn't want to stop. She wanted to feel this for him, even if it took her a while to put it all into words. They had time.

He kept pushing, his strong arms keeping his weight off her. Then he kissed her, a wild energy overtaking them both. His tongue dueled with hers, keeping her in the moment and making her forget the pain in her arm for a second. She pushed against him, feeling his warmth, letting herself get lost in everything that was Bosco. Finally, he pushed all the way inside, connecting them.

Something clicked. In her body, in her heart, maybe even deeper. She *felt* it. She felt him. Only him. Her eyes widened, and her lungs seized.

"Breathe," he whispered, his mouth against hers, his command firm.

She obeyed, letting her lungs take over. Relief filtered through her as oxygen flowed throughout her body again. This was intense, and she wanted more.

"Now." He levered up, using his elbows as balance, his pelvis flush against hers. "Want to call me an idiot again?" His voice was rough, and his tone gritty. His gaze was all-knowing and a little arrogant, but it suited him. Just like he suited her.

"No." She bit into his bottom lip. They could have all the chat time he wanted for pillow talk after he assuaged this desperate hunger inside her. "Later."

He licked his lip and then kissed her, pushing her head back into the pillow. Taking control. Pleasure swamped her, pushing her need for him even higher. She kissed him back, her hands frantic along his flanks. They were both breathing heavily when he lifted his head. "Now we talk," he murmured, his breath heating her lips.

Oh, he was going to kill her. She needed him to start moving before she exploded. This much need couldn't be healthy. What did he want? Oh, yeah. "Fine. You're not an idiot. Wait. You are. We aren't friends."

"Damn straight," he said, possession in his eyes, power in his body. "We're a hell of a lot more than friends, and we're going to give this a real shot. Got it?"

She'd gotten that a lot earlier than he had, but why quibble about it? "Yes," she breathed, tilting her hips.

He groaned, his jaw hardening.

She did it again, trying to ease the pleasurable pain of having him inside her, not moving. "You're big, Bosco. Start moving, would you?" she gasped.

He reached between them and fondled her breasts, the look in his eyes giving her pause. "You can take me." He distracted her for a moment, playing, taking his time as he seemed to like.

She scratched down his back to his butt and sank her nails in. Then she tilted again.

His nostrils flared, and he rose over her, grasping her hip and pulling out to push back in. She blinked. Then he went all-in. Fast and hard, he thrust into her, forcing her higher and higher before she could think of climbing. Each plunge of his hips pushed her into the mattress, so she wrapped her legs around him and just held on.

Live wires uncoiled inside her, and she cried out, grabbing on to him, her eyelids closing as sparks flashed behind them. The climax roared through her, taking her breath. Fireworks detonated one after the other, each harder and more spectacular until she could only feel. Finally, she came down, her mind numb. He slammed inside her one more time and stilled, jerking with his release.

Wow.

Finally, his body relaxed. His mouth wandered along her jawline, kissing beneath her ear. "You okay?"

"Not sure," she mumbled, her body so relaxed it was hard to catch a thought. "Might've passed out."

He chuckled and withdrew from her body, kissing her neck next to her bruise when she protested. "I'll be right back." He disappeared for a few moments and then returned to the bed to wrap his big body around hers. "I'm glad we reached an agreement."

"Ditto," she said, yawning. "But no more bossiness." Did she even mean that? Probably not. But a woman had to take a stand.

"I agree," he murmured. "Bossy doesn't suit you."

She blinked, snuggling into his warmth. "I meant you."

Glass shattered. Something clanked along the wooden floor in the living room. Bosco stiffened, covering her. "Grenade," he bellowed.

Chapter Twelve

Bosco knew the sound of a grenade, and that was it in the other room. He covered Marlie, his body flat over hers as the entire apartment exploded. The walls blasted in, and wooden slats from the floor flew up and then clattered back down, several scattering across his bed. Sheetrock and paint blew around, and his bookcase from the corner crashed down, his trophies shattering on the floor.

Fabio barked weakly from the other room. Was he hurt?

Boscoe's ears rang, and his vision wavered. A piece of the ceiling fell and broke across his shoulders, jolting him out of the darkness. Glass from the main light rained down, cutting his bare ass and clinking onto the floor.

He jumped from the bed, his shoulders burning, and headed right for the person coming through the window. He tossed the man back into the wall and watched him go down.

Two other masked figures barreled through the bedroom door, and Bosco pushed through the murky air to take down the first guy. One swipe, two punches, he let training take over and stopped thinking.

The other guy wasn't trained. However, he was masked and well-muscled, and he got in a couple of good shots with a knife.

Blood spurted across Bosco's chest, and pain cut through him. He shut down and stopped feeling. Growling, he reached for the guy's mask as Marlie screamed behind him.

Partially turning, he took a blade to the ribs. Agony shot through him, and he punched out, following with a kick that snapped the assailant's head back. The guy fell to the damaged floor, his hand flopping onto the wood and his legs kicking out, scattering snow from his boots.

A heavy object slammed down onto Bosco's skull, and he dropped to his knees, his vision going dark gray. Grunting, he shook his head, and blood slid into his eyes. He clutched the discarded knife off the floor, and pivoted to stab up and fast, cutting through a down jacket and into the second attacker's flesh. The guy's eyes widened behind the mask, he grabbed his stomach, and he dropped to his knees with a loud thunk.

The guy already on the floor kicked Bosco in the rib cage, and Bosco twisted on his knee, plunging the same knife into the bastard's gut. The assailant rolled at the last second, keeping the blade from causing internal damage. Even so, he screamed high and loud.

Marlie yelled from the doorway.

Bosco shoved to his feet just as the screaming guy did the same, finally shutting up. The guy Bosco had disabled by the window, his face covered by a gas mask, carried a furiously struggling Marlie across the room. She kicked wildly, her bare feet sliding off the torn wood. She looked terrified and way too fragile, buck-naked in the man's arms, fighting for all she was worth.

"Marlie!" Bosco yelled, just as the second guy punched him in the mouth. His jaw cracked, and his head snapped to the side, but he managed to stay on his feet. His mouth ached, but his teeth all remained in place. His ears ringing, his vision blurring, he went for the kill shot and punched the asshole in the throat.

Something popped.

The attacker fell again, this time his head hitting the wooden floor with the sound of a melon cracking. Bosco stumbled over the torn floor toward the doorway, which wavered dangerously in his sights.

The sound of Marlie screaming got farther away.

A dog barked and growled, fury and pain in the sound. "Get her, Fabio," Bosco croaked, his throat raw from the heated debris falling through the air. Blood flowed from him, over his naked body, and his feet burned as he tried to hurry toward the living room.

A shot echoed, and the dog yipped.

Marlie screamed louder, the sound high and frantic.

Bosco stumbled out of the bedroom to see Marlie fighting a man much bigger than her. The guy cut off her air, and she went limp, unconscious.

Then the man lifted his hand, pointing a black gun. Bosco tried to duck out of the way.

The guy fired.

Pain exploded in Bosco's chest, and he fell back, hitting the floor hard. The last sound he heard before the darkness grabbed him was Marlie screaming his name.

MARLIE REGAINED CONSCIOUSNESS SLOWLY, her body on high alert but her eyelids remaining shut. She breathed evenly and tried to take stock. The floor or ground was hard under a rough blanket beneath her, and a chill wound through the air. Quiet conversation took place to her right, male voices, but she couldn't make out the words.

Other than that, no sound filtered through the space.

She opened her eyelids, careful not to move from her position on her side. It took several heartbeats for her vision to clear enough to see the inside of a garage door in front of her.

"You're awake," a man said.

She rolled over, yanking the blanket up to cover her nude body, her bare butt on the cold cement. "Who are you?" She squinted, trying to see him better. The guy sat at a table near the other wall with a large blue truck behind him. He looked to be in his early thirties with brown hair, blue eyes, and all-black clothing. His gloves and mask were on the table.

"My name is Rickert. You've heard of me?" he asked.

"No." She put her back against the wall and looked around the large area. It was more than a garage. A metal shop? While the walls were blank, spots of gasoline marred the smooth concrete floor. "Why did you kidnap me?"

He winced. "Well, I had a question for you, but I think you just answered it."

She had never seen this guy in her entire life, nor had she heard of a Rickert. None of this made a lick of sense. Was it possible he had her confused with somebody else? "Did you break into my apartment the other night?"

"That was a colleague of mine." He shook his head. "After he failed so spectacularly, he's no longer with us."

Fear fissured through her. He'd killed his colleague? "I think you have me mixed up with somebody else," she murmured. How the heck was she going to get out of there? How long had she been unconscious? They couldn't be too far from town. She tilted her head and studied him.

An outside door to his side opened, and another man walked through.

She eyed him. Brown hair, brown eyes, normal build. His hands shook, and he shoved them into his pockets. She cleared her throat, trying to figure this out before somebody decided to shoot her. Wait a minute. He was familiar. Even so, she played dumb for the moment. "Who are you guys?"

The newcomer looked at the other guy and sighed. "Guess we worried about nothing."

There was something about his voice. Yep. That was him. He was one of the boring guys at the bar the other night. Her head hurt but she needed to concentrate. They'd stormed Bosco's apartment and kidnapped her, and she had no idea why. Bosco. Oh, God. Was he okay? "You shot Bosco," she said to Rickert. He was the bigger of the two, and he'd been the one to carry her out of the apartment after knocking her out. Was he the leader?

He nodded. "Yeah. He injured and possibly killed two of my friends. I hope he's dead."

Her chest hurt. She bit back tears and concentrated on the moment. Once she got out of here, she'd worry about Bosco. He was a trained soldier, and he had to be okay. Right now, considering these guys had let her see their faces, she was in trouble. Definite trouble. "Would one of you please tell me why you kidnapped me?" She tried not to feel too vulnerable, considering she only had the scratchy blanket to cover her nakedness. "This doesn't make sense."

"Yeah, sorry about that," the brown-haired guy said. She vaguely remembered him pattering on about numbers when she'd almost fallen asleep at the bar. With Turner. He looked at his partner. "This is a disaster, Rickert."

Rickert nodded. "We jumped the gun, that's for sure." He studied her. "Although we don't have much of a choice now, do we?" His gaze was hard and his jaw set.

She ran his name through her head again. It wasn't common. Shouldn't she know a Rickert? She looked at the man near the door. "I don't remember your name, but I do remember that you know Turner." Was he in on this? Or could he somehow help?

"Denny," Rickert said quickly. "I'm Rickert, and he's Denny."

Denny sucked in a breath, his face paling. "This is all Turner's fault."

"How so?" Marlie asked.

Denny pressed his lips together as if afraid to say too much.

Marlie squirmed on the cold floor. That was so not good. She'd seen their faces, and she knew their names. Apparently, Denny wasn't as comfortable ending her as was Rickert. He was definitely the weak link. She concentrated on him. "You kill me, and you'll go to hell, Denny." He turned even whiter. "Plus, let's be honest about this. Your friends, the ones Bosco hurt, are no doubt talking to the authorities right now and giving you up." If they were alive. It looked like at least one of them was killed. Her voice trembled, and she didn't try to hide her fear. Why bother?

Denny leaned back against the wall as if his legs wouldn't hold him up any longer.

She pressed on. "Right now, you've only gone along with a kidnapping. If you kill me, that's murder one. Do you really want to face the death penalty?" It was a good thing she loved watching *Law and Order*.

"Shut up," Rickert snapped.

She pulled the blanket more securely over her body, her mind finally kicking into gear. "Right now, your friends are giving you up. The police are checking all the surveillance cameras between Bosco's apartment and here, and even I know there are a couple of banks in that neighborhood. You're done. Best bet for both of you is to run while leaving me here and alive. Just in case you get caught." She listened in vain for sirens. Only the wind whipped against the outside of the metal walls.

Denny gagged and then quickly covered his mouth.

She pulled her legs in so she could jump to her feet if necessary. "Denny? You weren't one of the men in the apartment, were you?" Bosco had hurt two of them, and Rickert had carried her out. "You were just in the car. Waiting." He must have been the driver.

Denny nodded.

"Then you're okay," she whispered.

"No, he really isn't," Rickert said, pulling a gun from the back of his waist and shooting Denny in one smooth motion.

Denny's eyes widened as blood burst across his chest. He grabbed his shirt, pitched forward, and landed face-first on the floor. Blood flowed from beneath him to stain the concrete red.

Chapter Thirteen

B osco jerked awake in the emergency room just as Santa Claus slapped a bandage on his upper chest near his shoulder. "Santa?"

Santa wore a white lab coat that matched his long white beard and shorter hair. "Nope. Dr. Springfield here. You were shot near your clavicle, slashed across the ribs, and your earlier stitches were cut open. You have contusions and lacerations across your back and legs, and your feet have seen better days but don't need stitches. You're lucky to be alive."

Bosco forced himself back to reality. "Marlie." He tried to shove himself up.

"Whoa." Dr. Springfield put a heavy hand on his shoulder. "Hold on."

"Bosco? What happened?" Detective Pierce strode inside the room, wearing a faded T-shirt and old jeans as if he'd just gotten out of bed. His hair was ruffled and his jaw whiskered.

Bosco pushed the doctor away and sat, his head swimming from the pain. "They took Marlie. There was a grenade, and three guys breached my apartment."

Pierce nodded. "One is dead, and the other's being stitched up next door. The third is gone. As is Ms. Kreuk. Tell me everything."

He had to find her. Groaning, he turned his body so his bare feet touched the floor. "What are you doing to find her?"

"We're collecting all CCTV footage from the neighborhood as well as canvassing, but so far, nobody's seen anything," Pierce said. "Lie back down. You're in no condition to do anything."

"Bullshit." Bosco gingerly put weight on one foot.

A commotion sounded, and Rory shoved past a uniformed officer. "Bos. You okay?" Worry lit his glittering eyes.

"No." Bosco eyed his naked body. "I have to find her, Rory. She's out there." Fear, something foreign to him, blasted through his chest.

Rory slid a backpack off his shoulder to toss onto the bed. "Clothes in there. Fabio was shot in the leg but the vet easily stitched him up. Tessa is with him. Anna and Aiden are working the CCTV from the ATF's angle, and Aiden said he'd figure out how it's an ATF case later. As for our brothers, Vince and Finn are over the pass, preparing for a search and rescue in case the kidnappers went in that direction. Knox is outside, calling in favors in case we need to breach from the air. Well, he's calling in favors as you, to be honest."

His family was ready to go. Good. Bosco forced a T-shirt over his head and drew on some jeans, groaning when pain nearly dropped him, even though he was sitting.

"You shouldn't think of going anywhere," the doctor said, scooting away from the bed.

Bosco yanked on socks and a pair of boots that had been at the bottom of the bag. Wait a minute. "Where's Quint?" He was the only brother not mentioned.

Rory smiled, and the sight wasn't pretty. "Quint, who?"

Detective Pierce shoved away from the wall. "Damn it." He turned and hustled out into the hallway.

Bosco stood all the way, his breath catching at the pain.

Rory was instantly by his side. "You good?"

"Yeah." Bosco dug deep and hitched toward the doorway, his movements becoming more fluid. "Thanks for not arguing about my staying here."

"Please. Your woman has been kidnapped." Rory followed him into the hallway. "Turn right."

Raised voices came from two doors down, and Bosco increased his pace, limping into a room where Detective Pierce was trying to pull Quint off a patient on a bed. "What's happening?" he asked.

Quint stopped fighting the detective and straightened, flexing his hand. His brown eyes were pissed, and his shoulders were squared and ready to go. "I was just having a nice talk with this guy about why he blew up your apartment, and more importantly, about where Marlie might be."

Bosco nodded at his older brother and moved around Pierce, stopping short at seeing the bloody man on the examination table, his torso partially stitched up by a wide-eyed younger doctor. The laceration looked deep enough to need stitches but not bad enough to have caused internal damage. The guy must've been attacker number two—the one Bosco had stabbed. Bos moved up the bed and looked down at the guy's face. Wait a minute. "Turner?" Fury ripped through his ears, landing in his stomach. He planted a hand on Turner's shoulder. Hard. "What the hell?"

Turner's eyes were full of pain. His ripped down coat was in the corner, and tears filled his eyes. He coughed, and blood trickled from a split in his lip.

Detective Pierce tried to grab Bosco's arm, but Quint and Rory intercepted him, getting in his way. "I will arrest all three of you," Pierce snapped.

Bosco trusted his brothers to take care of Pierce. He leaned down and let his fury show. "Where is she?"

"I don't know," Turner said, a snot bubble sliding from his nose.

Bosco motioned the doctor back. "You're gonna want to

move, Doc." Then he flattened his hand over the still bleeding and open wound down Turner's torso, pressing down.

Turner gasped in pain, and his body stiffened. "God. Stop."

"No." Bosco twisted his hand, digging his fingers into the wound.

Turner cried out.

"Damn it," Detective Pierce yelled. "Bud, get in here."

Bud was probably the uniform that Bosco had seen in the hall. Bosco dug even deeper.

"She's in Rickert's shop," Turner gasped, his body shaking with pain. "They won't hurt her. They just want to make sure she won't say anything about the business."

A uniformed cop ran in, his chest big and broad. He headed for Bosco, but Detective Pierce waved him off.

"Who's Rickert, and where's his shop?" Detective Pierce growled.

Turner gasped, blood flowing from his gut. "The other night after the party, we were drunk at a bar across town. Just goofing off and not thinking. Denny and I started talking about Rickert's accounts, and I forgot that Marlie was even there. I don't think she was listening, but Denny told Rickert we'd discussed him, and the guy has guns, man. He threatened us."

"Daniel Rickert?" Detective Pierce snapped. "From McDougal's Accounting Firm?"

Bosco partially turned. "That ring a bell with you?"

"Yeah," Pierce said, reaching for his phone at his belt. "We've been investigating him for embezzlement for the last month."

Well, shit. "I need an address," Bosco snapped, heading for the door. "Now."

MARLIE WATCHED Rickert as he finished loading his truck with several suitcases while Denny bled on the floor. She wanted to check on him, but Rickert kept his gun pointed at her, promising to shoot her if she moved. Even so, she slowly stood, keeping her back to the wall and the blanket in front of her. The floor was piercing cold on her bare feet. She'd drop the blanket if she got the chance to attack him, but he was too far away.

He finally finished and looked at her, his gun hand level. "Come here."

She blinked. Her knees trembled, and her legs locked so she could jump out of the way if he fired. "Why?" The guy had just shot his friend, probably killed him. He would most likely want to kill her, as well.

"Insurance." He reached into the back of the truck and drew out what looked like regular rope. "Now. Don't forget that I will shoot you."

"I know," she whispered.

He motioned her. "I can just shoot you now, if you want."

"No." She moved toward him, tripping over the bottom of the blanket. Could she get the gun? He was bigger and not shaking from the cold like she was right now. Even so, she had to steal that weapon. She reached him.

"Hold out your hands," he said, an odd light in his eyes, the gun pointed at her chest.

She couldn't do that without letting go of the blanket. "You don't have to tie me up. I'll come with you."

"Hands. Now." He lifted the barrel and pointed it right at her face.

Her stomach lurched. Before she could drop the blanket, the door burst open, and three men rushed inside.

Rickert turned and fired at them.

She screamed and barreled into his shooting arm, smashing it against the truck. Strong arms grabbed her and yanked her away, and then she was off her feet and held against a muscular chest. The wrong chest. She looked up, shocked, as Rory Albertini squired her away from the gun and body on the floor to the other side of the shop, keeping her covered by the blanket.

She gasped and turned to see Bosco hit Rickert so hard he flew across the hood of the truck. "Bosco," she whispered.

He turned to look at her, a wild and furious glint in his topaz-colored eyes. Cuts, bruises, and bumps covered him. "You okay?"

Numbly, she nodded.

He rounded the truck, picked Rickert up by the neck, and slammed him down onto the metal so hard it dented.

"Enough," Detective Pierce ordered, not moving very quickly to stop him. He leaned over Denny and then rolled him, calling out. "We need an ambulance. Now." He leaned down to apparently listen for Denny's breathing. "Bosco? I mean it. Stop playing around."

Oh, Bosco wasn't playing. He lifted Rickert by the hair and threw him face-first into the wall. Rickert bounced back, flipped around, and caught a fist from Bosco in the gut. The sound of ribs breaking shattered the rough silence.

"Enough," Pierce bellowed, just as two uniformed officers ran into the shop followed by more men who looked a lot like Bosco.

Bosco let Rickert slide to the floor and calmly stepped over him, walking toward her. He reached them and gently ran his bruised knuckles across her cheekbone. "How badly are you hurt?" Lifting the blanket, he looked over her form while Rory kept his gaze on the uniformed officers behind him.

"I'm okay." Now that she was safe, tears gathered in her eyes. "I was so scared."

"I know." He gently lifted her out of Rory's arms, keeping the blanket in place and wincing.

She sucked in air. "You're hurt. Let me down."

"Never." He turned and strode past the police officers and what had to be his brothers to the misty night outside. "It happens fast with us Albertini brothers, you know." Ducking over her, he protected her from the pelting snow.

"So I've heard." She gave up trying to reason with him and just snuggled her face into the crook of his neck, breathing in his scent. Her body shook, probably from shock, and she let him protect her.

"Good." He opened the passenger side door of a silver truck and stepped up, keeping her on his lap. He shut the door, and heat blasted from the vents, warming her. "So, here it is. I know this is fast, and I'm more than willing to give you all the time in the world for us. We can date, we can court, we can go at your speed." He cuddled her closer, his heartbeat steady beneath her chin.

She blinked and looked over at the driver, who had black hair and twinkling greenish-blue eyes. "Hi."

"Hi. I'm Knox. Thanks for taking care of my dog." Knox grinned and put the truck in drive. "Are we headed to the hospital?"

"Yeah," Bosco said, settling her more comfortably on his lap. "I want to get her checked out, and I think my stitches popped again."

Knox drove away from the red and blue lights swirling from the emergency vehicles. "I'm sure the authorities will want to have another talk with you, anyway."

Now that she was safe, all sorts of aches and pains were springing to life on her body. But she couldn't get the sound of the gunshots out of her head. "What about Fabio?" she whispered. "He was so brave trying to save me, and Rickert shot him."

Knox smiled, watching the road. "Tess called. Fabio is doing well and will be released tomorrow."

Marlie sighed and relaxed against Bosco. She'd been so worried about the dog. "Oh. Okay." Relief buzzed through her. "So, courting, huh?" Sounded good.

"Yeah," Bosco breathed. "I figure we'll get married in the spring."

Knox laughed out loud.

Chapter Fourteen

B osco settled Marlie on Nonna's sofa while family members milled around, and at least two of his brothers kept spiking the punch over on the main table. Of course, the family knew it was spiked, so everyone kept the kids away from that bowl. Christmas music wafted throughout the space from hidden speakers, and the family was spread throughout the entire house, all eating, drinking, or goofing off. It was good to be home.

Marlie looked delectable in a red sweater and black slacks, a glass of red wine in her hand. Her arm was still bandaged but she was moving with ease even though she had to be sore from the explosion. "You are going to have to stop hovering over me." She was cute, but even she didn't sound like she believed that.

He stretched out next to her as two of his younger cousins rolled around near the tree, wrestling. "Nonna is gonna kill you two if you knock over that tree again," he called out. Although it wasn't like he hadn't done the same thing at their age.

A bark sounded, and Fabio bounded over, his right leg bandaged.

"Fabio!" Marlie cried, setting her glass down and reaching for the huge mutt.

The dog jumped into her lap, skidding until his face hit Bosco's healthy shoulder. Marlie wrapped both arms around him and snuggled her face into his fur. "You are so brave." She let him flop down on both of their laps, holding on tightly.

Bosco sighed and gave the dog a look.

The canine really did seem to smile.

Knox rounded the corner, a plate of food in his hand. "Oops. Sorry about that. Want me to make him move?"

"No," Marlie said, petting the dog's ears. "He can stay right here." She looked too happy for Bosco to force the dog onto the floor. "He's the bravest dog in the entire world."

The canine panted happily, no doubt in agreement.

Knox chuckled and sat on the sofa table, facing them. "I called Detective Pierce for an update. Turner, Denny, and Rickert are all alive and in the hospital, facing charges. Looks like they're going to survive to spend a lot of years in prison. Jackasses."

Marlie shook her head. "It's all so weird. I was so bored on that date with Turner that I really didn't listen to a thing they said at that bar."

The oldest brother, Vince, poked his head around the corner. "Knox? I need backup. Rory is heading out to kidnap Serenity right now, but he said he'd give her until the new year. It's not the new year yet." He disappeared.

Knox set his food down. "I'll be back." Then he stood and hustled after his brother.

Marlie watched them go. "Um, he seemed more concerned that the kidnapping was happening early than it was happening at all." She reached for a piece of celery from Knox's plate.

Man, she fit right in.

Bosco slid an arm over her shoulders. "Don't worry about them. I wanted to tell you that I plan to put in for a transfer first thing next week. Maybe something on the ground here."

She looked up, her eyes narrowing. "Don't even think about it.

You love your job and shouldn't change that for anybody. I can handle it, Bos."

He studied her earnest expression, his chest lightening. She really meant it. His heart thumped. All hers. Oh, it was probably way too early to tell her how he felt, but she did understand the Albertini guys. "So. We gonna move in together?"

She chuckled. "It's a little early for that, don't you think?"

Yeah, but his heart was gone. All hers. "Sure. We can take all the time you want." Of course, they'd be staying together. He'd never forget the sight of her being kidnapped from his apartment. It might take a while to feel comfortable not being next to her, offering protection. Plus, it'd take months to repair his apartment. "When we fall, we fall hard and fast." He leaned over and kissed her, going deep. "I love you. Just thought you should know." He grinned.

Life was so damn good.

MARLIE COULD BARELY BREATHE. Man, he could kiss. Apparently, he had no problem sharing feelings because he'd just laid it out there. It was way too early to declare love, much less feel it. Still... She chuckled. "I love you, too." Oh, she shouldn't. Not yet anyway. Maybe it was the kidnapping and shootings and all the action surrounding them, but she didn't feel like hiding anything. "But it is too early. We are going to date and court and all of that, Bosco Albertini."

"Sure thing." He snagged a drumstick off Knox's plate just as his brother Quint walked into the room, holding hands with a lovely blonde, a black Labrador following them. She'd met Quint at the hospital after her kidnapping, and he seemed sweet if a little dangerous. Well, like the Albertini's in general, it appeared.

Quint grinned. "Marlie, I wanted you to meet Heather."

"Hi," Heather said, sitting in the adjacent chair with the dog flattening herself over her feet. "Welcome to chaos."

Marlie laughed. "Thanks. That's not the first time I've heard that. It's nice to meet you." The couple looked right together, and hadn't they only dated for a couple of weeks? A toddler crawled beneath Marlie's legs, and she lifted them, letting him go on by.

Heather watched the little boy. "You get used to the wildness of the family?" She sounded a bit unsure.

Quint kissed her on the cheek, and she turned a lovely pink. "Who knows. At the very least, you learn to survive it," he rumbled.

"Isn't this nice?" Nonna Albertini bustled in and refilled both Marlie's and Heather's wine glasses. "It's so lovely to have you two here. Thank you for bringing goodies." She wore a dark green dress that cinched in at her small waist and had her thick hair piled on her head. "Now, boys. Would you please go stop Knox and Vince? They're causing problems with Rory, and your father doesn't seem interested in getting involved. Your mother is helping with the turkey."

Marlie swirled her wine in her glass. "I thought Knox and Vince were preventing a kidnapping."

Nonna waved her hand in the air. "No. Rory and Serenity need to talk, and if they have to go to the cabin to do so, then that's okay. Kidnapping isn't the correct term."

Bosco's eyebrows rose. "Nonna, I don't think you should encourage Rory."

"Pssh," Nonna said, glancing toward the doorway. "Oh. There's Anna. She'll help me." She bustled off.

Quint sighed and took the seat next to Heather. "She's not going to be happy until she marries us all off. I heard her tell Mom that Vince is next, and she has somebody in mind for him."

Marlie settled against Bosco's supportive arm draped across her shoulders. The family vibe felt good, and she was starting to sink into it. Someday, if Rory wasn't arrested, she'd ask him to tell her the story about Serenity. For now, she just wanted to relax and enjoy the hot-bodied hero next to her. She'd never forget the sight of him running into that shop, injured, with the barrel of a gun pointed at him.

He tugged on her ear. "What are you thinking about?"

She grinned. "Just about forever."

Yeah. Forever. They had that, and it started right now.

Epilogue

Anna Albertini barely kept her nonna from shooing Vince and Knox away from Rory. "Nonna, trust me. Rory gave her until after the new year, and he has to keep his word. You know that."

Her grandmother rolled her eyes and headed back into the kitchen, where it looked as if the roast might be burning.

Tessa slid up to her side. "Nice job. If we keep her concentrated on Rory, then she won't come after us."

Anna grinned at her older sister. "That's the thought."

Tessa's reddish-blond hair was in an intricate braid, bringing out the definition in her stunning face. "Where is Aiden, anyway?"

Even the mention of his name made Anna's insides go squishy. "He's helping Dad shovel the front walk again since the snow is coming down so hard." He wasn't exactly happy with her right now, but she'd made a commitment on a legal case, and she couldn't go back on her word. Plus, irritated sex with Aiden often got wild, and she couldn't complain about that.

Donna, their oldest sister, moved in their direction from the kitchen. She was a younger version of Nonna and wore a green sweater with her lighter pants. "Get that goofy smile off your face.

I can tell you're thinking smexy things about Aiden." She handed a glass of wine to both of them.

Anna laughed, looking into the living room where Quint sat next to Heather, and Bosco kept playing with Marlie's hair. "Isn't it interesting how fast those two fell? I mean, I've heard the rumors of the Albertini men falling at first sight, but to see it in action is pretty amazing." Although both couples looked happy, and they fit perfectly.

"I know," Donna whispered, lifting her wineglass to her mouth. "I have to say that I love both Marlie and Heather already. They've made our cousins so happy. I've never seen Bosco so relaxed, and the guy is full of stitches right now."

Anna chuckled.

Tessa glanced at her. "How's the Santa case coming?"

"It's finished, and I properly kept Santa out of prison," Anna retorted.

"Is Aiden still all overprotective about you being injured? Again?" Donna asked, just as the front door opened, and their dad and Aiden walked in.

Anna nodded, watching Aiden. His too-blue gaze scanned the room and landed on her—like always. "There's a lot going on right now, but we're solid."

He smiled, and her heart flipped over.

Oh, they were so much more than solid. They were everything. She smiled back and then moved toward him, leaning up to kiss him. The holidays were for love and family, and she was surrounded by both.

For now, she'd take this moment and enjoy it.

Tomorrow could come tomorrow.

***

I hope you enjoyed this glimpse into the Albertini family! If you're interested in more, take a look at Anna's first full novel, Disorderly Conduct. Here's a quick excerpt for you:

"You don't." In a shift of muscle, Aiden plucked me right off the ground to sit on the hood of my car.

The air sliced all funny in my chest, and I gaped at him. "What are you doing?"

He leaned in; his hands planted on either side of my hips. "Showing you that you're totally out of your depth. You're in the middle of nowhere with a guy out on felony bond after having left a club business where fifteen guys would provide an alibi if I needed one." His head jerked slightly toward the car. "Do you even have a gun in there?"

"Always." I probably should've been scared, because every word he'd said was true. But I wasn't. Oh, my entire central nervous system misfired like a supernova, but none of that was fear. Maybe a dollop of caution with a whole boatload of curiosity. "You won't hurt me."

His nostrils flared and he straightened. "Damn it." This close, his eyes were a myriad of different blue hues. "I won't hurt you, but I can't keep you from being hurt. What we do—this is too big to protect anyone so nosy. Just trust me."

I couldn't answer him, because I was going to try and save him if possible. First, I needed facts. "Tell me the whole story."

"No." He looked me over, head to toe, his gaze penetrating.

I tried not to squirm, knowing I was totally losing this staring contest.

Then he shocked me by running both hands through my hair and messing it up more. His touch was slightly rough with a whole lot of heat.

"What are you doing?" I swatted his hands away.

He leaned back and studied me again before twisting the neckline of my T-shirt. His calloused fingers brushed the bare skin of my chest, and I couldn't help a shiver. The caress danced down my skin with a wave of heat.

I slapped him again. "What the hell?"

"The guys don't know who you are, but if they ever do, I'd

rather they think we were out here fuckin' and not talkin'," he muttered, checking over the rest of me.

Heat blazed into my cheeks. "Oh, for goodness sakes." The idea of sex with Aiden was one I'd had over the years. That was imaginary Aiden and not this real-life devil. Truth be told, I wasn't sure I could handle him. I glanced down at my twisted shirt. "Happy now?"

He stepped back and looked me over, his mouth pursing. "No."

Then, against all possibilities, he moved back in, his rough palm skimming along my jaw. I started to argue, and his mouth covered mine.

Shock blasted through me followed by a wave of heat. His thumb pressed against my jaw, and I opened my mouth. He swept in, kissing me, pushing me so I had to struggle to keep from falling back onto the hood. Every kiss I'd ever had, even in law school, pooled into memories of a girl kissing a boy.

This moment was all man kissing woman.

I groaned low, kissing him back, arousal zinging through me faster than I would've ever thought possible. He went even deeper, and I completely lost myself in him.

Then he released me.

I gasped for air, my mind fuzzing, my body wide awake and ready to go.

He ran a thumb over my still tingling and no doubt swollen bottom lip. "Now I'm happy," he murmured, his eyes an unfathomable blue and his expression unreadable. "You can drive me back now."

Get your copy of Disorderly Conduct today.

Acknowledgments

Thank you to:

Tony, Gabe, and Karlina for being such a fun and supportive family;

Asha Hossain of Asha Hossain Designs, LLC for the fantastic cover;

Chelle Olson of Literally Addicted to Detail for the wonderful edits;

Stella Bloom for the perfectly pitched narration for the audio books;

Liz Berry, Jillian Stein, Asa Maria Bradley, and Boone Brux for the advice with the concepts for this new series;

Caitlin Blasdell, for being my incredibly hard working agent;

Anissa Beatty, for your hard work as my perfectly organized assistant and for being such a great leader for Rebecca's Rebels (my FB street team);

Thanks to Rebels Heather Frost, Kimberly Frost, Madison Fairbanks, Suzi Zuber, Asmaa Nada Qayyum, Leanna Feazel, Joan Lai, Jessica Mobbs, Karen Clementi, and Karen Fisher for their assistance.

Thank you to Writer Space and Fresh Fiction PR for all the hard work. Thank you also to my constant support system: Gail and Jim English, Kathy and Herbie Zanetti, Debbie and Travis Smith, Stephanie and Don West, Jessica and Jonah Namson and Chelli and Jason Younker.

Reading Order of each Series

I know many of you like the exact reading order for each series, so here they are as of the release of this book, although if you read most novels out of order, it's okay.

THE ANNA ALBERTINI FILES

1. Disorderly Conduct (Book 1)
2. Bailed Out (Book 2)
3. Adverse Possession (Book 3)
4. Holiday Rescue novella (Novella 3.5)
5. Santa's Subpoena (Book 4)
6. Holiday Rogue (Novella 4.5)
7. Tessa's Trust (Book 5)
8. Holiday Rebel (Novella 5.5)
9. Habeas Corpus (Book 6)

GRIMM BARGAINS

1. One Cursed Rose (Book 1)

LAUREL SNOW SERIES

1. You Can Run (Book 1)
2. You Can Hide (Book 2)
3. You Can Die (Book 3)
4. You Can Kill (Book 4) - 2024

DEEP OPS SERIES

1. Hidden (Book 1)
2. Taken Novella (Book 1.5)
3. Fallen (Book 2)
4. Shaken (in Pivot Anthology) (2.5)
5. Broken (Book 3)
6. Driven (Book 4)
7. Unforgiven (Book 5)
8. Frostbitten (Book 6)
9. Unforgotten (Book 7) - TBA
10. Deep Ops # 8 - TBA

Redemption, WY

1. Rescue Cowboy Style (Novella in the Lone Wolf Anthology)
2. Rescue Hero Style (Novella in the Peril Anthology)
3. Rescue Rancher Style (Novella in the Cowboy Anthology)
4. Book # 1 launch - subscribe to my newsletter for more information about the new series.

Dark Protectors

1. Fated (Dark Protectors Book 1)
2. Claimed (Dark Protectors Book 2)
3. Tempted Novella (Dark Protectors 2.5)
4. Hunted (Dark Protectors Book 3)
5. Consumed (Dark Protectors Book 4)
6. Provoked (Dark Protectors Book 5)
7. Twisted Novella (Dark Protectors 5.5)
8. Shadowed (Dark Protectors Book 6)
9. Tamed Novella (Dark Protectors 6.5)
10. Marked (Dark Protectors Book 7)
11. Wicked Ride (Realm Enforcers 1)
12. Wicked Edge (Realm Enforcers 2)
13. Wicked Burn (Realm Enforcers 3)
14. Talen Novella (Dark Protectors 7.5)
15. Wicked Kiss (Realm Enforcers 4)
16. Wicked Bite (Realm Enforcers 5)
17. Teased (Reese -1001 DN Novella)
18. Tricked (Reese-1001 DN Novella)
19. Tangled (Reese-1001 DN Novella)
20. Vampire's Faith (Dark Protectors 8) *****VF is a great entry point for series, if you want to start here*****
21. Demon's Mercy (Dark Protectors 9)
22. Vengeance (Rebels 1001 DN Novella)
23. Alpha's Promise (Dark Protectors 10)
24. Hero's Haven (Dark Protectors 11)
25. Vixen (Rebels 1001 DN Novella)
26. Guardian's Grace (Dark Protectors 12)
27. Vampire (Rebels-1001 DN)
28. Rebel's Karma (Dark Protectors 13)
29. Immortal's Honor (Dark Protector 14)
30. A Vampire's Kiss (Rebels-1000 DN)
31. Garrett's Destiny (Dark Protectors 15)
32. Warrior's Hope (Dark Protectors 16)

33. A Vampire's Mate (Rebels-1000 DN)
34. Prince of Darkness (DP 17) 2024
35. Eye of the Cat (DP 18) 2024
36. Heart of the Hunter (DP 19)

STOPE PACKS (wolf shifters)

1. Wolf
2. Alpha
3. Shifter

SIN BROTHERS/BLOOD BROTHERS

1. Forgotten Sins (Sin Brothers 1)
2. Sweet Revenge (Sin Brothers 2)
3. Blind Faith (Sin Brothers 3)
4. Total Surrender (Sin Brothers 4)
5. Deadly Silence (Blood Brothers 1)
6. Lethal Lies (Blood Brothers 2)
7. Twisted Truths (Blood Brothers 3)

SCORPIUS SYNDROME SERIES

**This is technically the right timeline, but I'd always meant for the series to start with Mercury Striking.

Scorpius Syndrome/The Brigade Novellas

1. Scorpius Rising
2. Blaze Erupting
3. Power Surging - TBA
4. Hunter Advancing - TBA

Scorpius Syndrome NOVELS

1. Mercury Striking (Scorpius 1)

2. Shadow Falling (Scorpius 2)
3. Justice Ascending (Scorpius 3)
4. Storm Gathering (Scorpius 4)
5. Winter Igniting (Scorpius 5)
6. Knight Awakening (Scorpius 6)

About the Author

New York Times and *USA Today bestselling* author Rebecca Zanetti has published more than fifty romantic-suspense and dark paranormal novels, which have been translated into several languages, with millions of copies sold world-wide. Her books have received Publisher's Weekly starred reviews, won RT Reviewer Choice awards, have been featured in Entertainment Weekly, Woman's World and Women's Day Magazines, have been included in retailer's best books of the year, and have been favorably reviewed in both the Washington Post and the New York Times Book Reviews. Rebecca has ridden in a locked Chevy trunk, has asked the unfortunate delivery guy to release her from a set of handcuffs, and has discovered the best silver mine shafts in which to bury a body...all in the name of research. Honest. Find Rebecca at: www.RebeccaZanetti.com